D0242153

Truth or Dare

Celia Rees lives in Leamington Spa, Warwickshire, with her
husband and teenage daughter. She taught English in city com-
prehensive schools for seventeen years, and now divides her
time between writing, talking to readers in schools and
libraries, and teaching creative writing on the University of
Warwick's Open Studies Programme.

She writes for older children and teenagers and her books have
wide popular appeal, combining compelling story-telling with
powerful themes and subject matter.

*Truth or Dare* won the Stockport Children's Book Award and
was shortlisted for the NASEN Special Needs Children's Book
Award, the Angus Book Award and the Sheffield Children's
Book Award.

*Books by Celia Rees*

Truth or Dare
The Bailey Game
Colour Her Dead
Midnight Hour

## What critics have said about *Truth or Dare*

'With computer games and Fifties flashbacks, *Truth or Dare* doesn't let up – and hits you with a final twist.'
*Daily Telegraph*

'*Truth or Dare* is an unsettling, unputdownable mystery. The novel skillfully evokes late 1950s childhood – both the idyllic freedom enjoyed by the well-adjusted child, and the damage suffered by others as a consequence of ignorance about autistic spectrum disorders.'
*TES*

'This is a compelling story in which the secrecy and shame of the past are shed to reveal a rather wonderful and utterly contemporary present. It also presents the challenges faced by people with Asperger's Syndrome, and their families, in a sensitive and enlightening way.'
*The Scotsman*

'In threading the narrative strands together, Rees recounts a terrible human tragedy…This is a compelling examination of the wreckage resulting from a determination to force conformity on an individual.'
Lindsey Fraser, *Children's Book of the Week*, *The Guardian*

'The sense of mystery is irresistible and, best and rarest of all, the explanation lives up to the mystery.'
*Independent on Sunday*

'Celia Rees's *Truth or Dare* is a detective story: Josh uncovers the truth about his uncle – and a terrible secret bubbles up through his mother's own memories. A moving book that puts autism a little more firmly on the teenager map.'
Sarah Johnson, *The Times*

'Cutting between past and present, this suspenseful, intriguing story is equally at ease with computer games and SF comics. Rees is a cunning author; respect her!'
*The Independent*

'This is a very good book, skillfully multi-layered, unputdownable and finally, very moving and thought-provoking.'
*Books for Keeps*

# TRUTH
# OR DARE

## Celia Rees

**MACMILLAN**
**CHILDREN'S BOOKS**

First published 2000 by Macmillan Children's Books

This edition published 2000 by Macmillan Children's Books
a division of Macmillan Publishers Limited
20 New Wharf Road, London N1 9RR
Basingstoke and Oxford
www.panmacmillan.com

Associated companies throughout the world

ISBN 0 330 36875 3

17  19  18  16

A CIP catalogue record for this book is available from
the British Library.

Typeset by SX Composing DTP, Rayleigh, Essex
Printed and bound in Great Britain by Mackays of Chatham plc, Kent

*Thanks to Judith and Andy for all the different kinds of help
and advice that they gave me.*

*For Roy*

# Chapter 1

The last place Joshua Parker wanted to be on a sunny day in late July was sitting in a car, stuck in heavy traffic, heading north on the M1. Cars towing trailers and caravans clogged the lane in front, almost bringing it to a standstill. Holiday traffic. But Josh was not going on holiday. He was being driven away from his friends, his summer, kidnapped by his own mother.

He glanced over to the driver's seat, where his mother sat, her face frowning and tense, her fingers drumming the steering wheel. It was hot in here, and stuffy. The car was packed with gear. They were going to stay at his grandmother's for an indefinite period. Josh did not like going there, even in the best of circumstances.

His mother stared forward, unresponsive, so Josh turned away again, studying the road ahead. The traffic was freeing up now. The speedo flickered through 50, to 60, and 70, climbing steadily. The cars and lorries kept pace with each other as they travelled towards a point where the motorway narrowed. It was almost like entering a tunnel. Huge landscaped escarpments reared up on either side, cutting the sky down to a slot of blue. The three lanes were squeezed down, causing the traffic to bunch as the stream of vehicles entered the deep defile.

Josh was still reviewing his grievances, safe in his metal cocoon, when all his problems went right out of his head. He was a fraction of a second away from death.

Suddenly, without any kind of warning, their car swerved violently, veering into the outside lane. The cars there were doing 80, 90 miles per hour and were practically nose to tail. Josh's stomach lurched and he sat frozen, gripping his seat. Everything seemed to slow as traffic juggled and slewed, brakes squealing, horns blaring. Car lights flashed in furious warning; drivers mouthed curses through Plexiglas, faces white with their own fear. Josh's mother wrenched the wheel, this way, that way, sending her small car pin-balling back across the carriageway. There was a sharp hiss, and a deep braying hoot as a juggernaut fish-tailed past them, missing their bumper by millimetres. She dodged into the inside lane, just making the space between a four wheel drive and a transit, braking sharply to avoid rear-ending the van. The bag of game CDs shot off the back seat, landing with a crashing slither. Mum's boxed computer, lodged next to it, slammed Josh a good one right in the kidneys.

'Mum!' Josh screamed, his voice travelling up a full octave. 'What d'you think you're doing!'

'I thought I saw something . . .' his mother said.

'Where?' Josh asked, his voice returning to its newly acquired bass range.

'Back there.'

Josh squinted in the wing mirror at the receding motorway, trying to work out what could possibly have made her swerve like that. There was something flapping high up, caught in the wire fence that ran along the top of the embankment. A fertilizer bag perhaps, wafted by the updraft from the constant flow of traffic below. Nothing to be alarmed about. He glanced back at his mother. She was not generally a nervous driver.

'We used to play here,' she said, her voice strange, muffled and oddly vague. 'Before they built the motorway. I had forgotten. Completely forgotten.'

Although it was stiflingly hot in the car, his mother shivered and the fine hairs rose on her arms.

'Something walking on my grave,' she said, taking one hand off the wheel to rub at the ridged flesh. She bit her lip, held it caught between her front teeth, and laughed to herself. The sound she made was somewhere between a giggle and a sob. 'Sorry if I scared you, Josh.'

The traffic had slowed to a crawl again. Josh grunted and stared straight ahead, waiting for his heartbeat to ease up a bit. He didn't trust himself to speak. After a while he relaxed back in his seat, putting her weird behaviour down to worry about Gran.

'You've got to help now, Josh,' he could hear Dad saying. 'You're not a little boy any more.'

At thirteen he considered himself nearly grown up, but was still little boy enough to feel the injustice. Dad wasn't here, was he? Neither was Maggie. She was four years older, and she was a girl. She was the one who ought to be here, not Joshua. Truth was neither of them wanted to come with Mum, but they had excuses so they could get out of it. Dad could not take the time off work. Maggie had gone on holiday with her mates. Which left Joshua. Dad's job took him away from home; Josh was too young to be left on his own, and so . . .

The traffic was thinning out. His mother seemed more or less in control as she shifted into a higher gear and the car picked up speed. A sign for their turn-off loomed up and passed. Every turn of the wheels was bringing them nearer to their destination. His grandmother's house. Josh shivered, goosebumps travelling up under the sleeves of his T-shirt at the thought of it. There was something about the big tall house that gave him the creeps. It was always dark, even on a bright day like this, and cold, and it smelt of boiled fish.

Josh had not been back there since early spring. There had been a big family party to mark his grandmother's eightieth birthday. It had all been too much for her. About halfway through the celebrations, Josh had found her slumped on the stairs, frail hands clutching the banister.

'I've just got to have a little sit down,' she'd said, her voice slurring, her pale blue eyes, blank, unfocused, staring up at him.

'Not here, Gran,' he'd said, reaching down to her. 'This isn't a good place. Let me help you up.'

For one awful moment he thought she might be drunk. Then her head lolled and the side of her face seemed to slip downwards; her eyes rolled up in her head and she started to breathe in a strange way. Josh had looked round in panic. It brought him out in a sweat just thinking about it. He'd wanted to back away, pretend he hadn't been there, hadn't seen her.

But he didn't. He called for help instead and bent down, preparing to lift her.

When the ambulance came, Mum and Uncle Paul went off with Gran. Most of the guests had stayed on. Subdued now, but still eating and drinking, talking about strokes and brain haemorrhages instead of holidays and gardens.

Their diagnosis had been confirmed by the hospital. A mild stroke they said, and she'd been kept in for observation. She'd seemed all right that time, and had been allowed home, but two weeks last Sunday it had happened again. She had been taken back to hospital and kept in, because this attack had been more serious. But now she was due to come out. Although recovered enough to leave the ward, she could not cope on her own. Grandpa had died years ago, there was no one at home to help her. She would need someone, for a while at least, until she got back on her feet. That was where Mum came in. She had volunteered. She would not consign her mother to the care of strangers. It was her duty to look after her. Josh understood this; he had endured the talks about how would he like it, lying in a bed, helpless, cared for by people you didn't even know . . .

A branching arrow pointed to the slip road. Josh sneaked a look over at his mother to see how she was doing now.

'Nearly home,' she said.

Josh did not reply as she indicated left, just nodded and turned his eyes to the front. She was using that strange voice again. She's tense, he told himself, worrying about Gran, she's been under a strain. But nothing he could think of quite explained her actions away. The sudden swerve for no reason, followed by the distant look on her face. He was glad that they were nearly there. Her slow movements and dreamy voice were scaring him far more than had the flashing lights, the squealing brakes and screaming horns of their near-collision.

# Chapter 2

Gran's house was a solid, redbrick, semi-detached Edwardian villa situated off the main road in a looping cul-de-sac. When his mother was a child this had been on the edge of the countryside, but since then the small market town had grown considerably. Green fields had been built over with bypasses, warehouses, out-of-town shopping areas. New estates and houses packed the spaces between the ribbon roads of older developments.

Gran's house had attic rooms and cellars. The garden was long, with sheds and unexpected overgrown places which invited exploration and spoke of possibilities. It used to remind Josh of the houses in old style children's adventure books: *Just William*, and Enid Blyton's stories. The kind of house where you would wake up in the morning and just know that something exciting was going to happen. But nothing ever did and he had grown out of expecting it on their infrequent visits.

Maybe something would happen this time, Josh thought as he got his gear out of the car. On the whole, it seemed unlikely. He was too old now and you need friends for adventures, a gang, and Josh had no friends here.

There was a girl next door. Katherine. Josh remembered her name from Gran's party. She was very pretty, slim, not very tall, with shoulder length browny-blonde hair. But she was older than him, fifteen or sixteen. She had spent the time at the party being chatted up by Barry and John, Uncle Paul's sons, who were seventeen and nineteen. Josh sighed. She'd be like Maggie and her friends: looking at him like he was some kind of pond slime. He glanced up at the neighbouring house, just in case, but there was no sign of anyone. He was heading for a lonely time. Lonely and boring.

The house smelt of lavender, not fish anymore. Mrs Reynolds, Gran's neighbour on the other side, had been in to make things ready. Gran wasn't home yet, she was not expected until later. Mother and son stood together under the slow ticking clock, caught in the silence of the empty house. To Joshua, it was like walking into another age, full of heavy wooden furniture and big ornate mirrors. A hall stand bristled with walking sticks and umbrellas whose owners would never use them now. The highly polished table held a dinner gong and a strange collection of souvenirs and knick-knacks: 'Present from Torquay', little china ornaments. It felt like stepping into a museum exhibition. His mother's face had a frozen blank expression. She looked like someone walking back into prison.

'Yoo-hoo, it's only me!' A voice called out behind them.

Mrs Reynolds was coming in through the door. She must have been watching for their arrival from behind her lacy net curtains.

8

Mrs Reynolds was Gran's oldest friend. They had moved in at the same time, young women, just married. They had been young mums together. Now their children had long ago grown up and left, and both their husbands were dead. Mrs Reynolds was one of the few people left from 'the old days' when everything was magic. The time when the town had 'real shops', and 'this was all country' and there wasn't 'all this traffic'. 'The new neighbours' were nice enough, Gran would explain, but not like 'the old crowd'. 'The new neighbours', as far as Josh could see, consisted of anyone who had moved in since 1970. 'The old crowd' had either died or moved away, all except Mrs Reynolds.

'Joanna! I'm so glad to see you.' She took the younger woman's hands and gave them a squeeze. 'I've been popping in, keeping an eye on things, keeping it nice for her.'

Joanna Parker murmured her thanks but Mrs Reynolds' attention had already turned to Joshua.

'My, you *have* grown!' she exclaimed, patting his hand. 'Even since the last time I saw you!'

Mrs Reynolds was as old as Gran, but she seemed much younger. She was slim and straight-backed, dressed in lime green slacks and a thick knit cardigan jacket. She wore pinky-orange lipstick which crept up and down into the tiny creases round her lips and a thin cobwebby mist of dyed black hair haloed a face thickly coated with powder.

'Regularly shooting up.' She peered at him, her dark eyes bright and alert, outlined and shadowed in blue, like some kind of exotic bird. 'Quite the young man.

You're going to be as tall as your father. Don't you think so, Joanna?'

'Umm, yes.' His mother looked at her watch and Mrs Reynolds smiled.

'I know, I know, don't let me rattle on. Your mind's on more than the growth potential of your son. Your mum'll be here soon, we'd better be getting things ready.'

They followed Mrs Reynolds up to the first landing. Gran's room was at the back of the house. Joanna was to have the guest room at the front. Josh was supposed to have the little room next to it.

'I thought Josh might go in here.'

Josh looked in with nose-wrinkling disgust at a space the size of a guinea pig cage. There wasn't enough room for him, let alone his stuff. There wasn't even a proper bed, just some kind of put-u-up. Plus it smelt a bit like a guinea pig cage: hot, airless and musty.

'Now, Josh,' his mother said, interpreting the signs. 'Please don't start making a fuss.'

'I'm not making a fuss. There's just no way I'm going to sleep in there.' He stood back, arms folded, matter-of-fact. He nodded to a short flight of stairs which led to the second landing. 'Why can't I go up there? Mum's old room, or Uncle Paul's?'

Mrs Reynolds shook her head. 'Those rooms are rather packed, I'm afraid. Your gran tends not to use the top of the house.' She looked across at Joanna. 'They are still full of stuff left over from when your dad died. I've been encouraging her to have a good clear out, but . . .'

Joanna nodded. She understood. Her mother could

10

never bear to part with anything. 'You never know when it might come in useful'. When it all got too much, she'd shut the door on it rather than sort it out.

'What about the attic?' Josh asked.

'Patrick's room?'

His mum and Mrs Reynolds looked at each other.

'It hasn't been used since . . .' Joanna left the sentence unfinished. 'It'll be awfully messy and dusty,' she added quickly. 'I don't think it's a good idea.'

'I'll sort it out. I can dust . . . and vacuum . . .'

'That'll be a first.' She smiled over at Mrs Reynolds.

'Just because I don't do it that much,' Josh said, stung by their adult collusion. 'Doesn't mean I don't know how.'

'Let him, Joanna,' Mrs Reynolds intervened, smoothing the waters. 'It will mean less disturbance if your mother wakes, if you have to go to her in the night.'

Josh looked over at the old lady, grateful for her support. It was just a room switch after all, what was the big deal? He watched the different expressions flit across his mother's face and prepared himself for another refusal, but in the end she said:

'All right. But check the next landing first. I still think it'd be better to use one of the rooms up there.'

'If you do need to clean,' Mrs Reynolds added, 'the dusters and bin bags are in the kitchen under the sink and the vacuum's in the cubby hole under the stairs.'

Mrs Reynolds was right. Both the rooms on the next landing were crammed floor to ceiling, with hardly room to stand, let alone walk about between the mattresses stacked against the wall and the old pieces of furniture.

Uncle Paul's room still had his name on the door. A little faded plaque he must have made in Woodwork. Josh fought his way round a ring of high-backed chairs, thin on the arms, that clustered round a coffee table topped with cracked glass and piled high with lethal electrical appliances, broken irons, and different kinds of fires. This was the place for the things which could not be thrown away, but could not go on display: all the mistakes, the worn, the faulty, the sins of the house banished to the upper storeys. Including Grandpa, it seemed.

There were suitcases full of his clothes. Model boats, broken masted and rigged with cobwebs, leaned against boxes of other stuff: bits of old uniform, a military cap he must have worn in the war, all kinds of other military memorabilia, and books. Josh blew the dust off boring looking hardbacks, bound in drab dark blue and olive green, volumes of military history.

Grandpa had died when Josh was quite a little child. Too young to remember him clearly, Josh recalled him now in a series of snapshots. A big man who seemed bent over with a rim of white hair around his shiny bald skull. Josh remembered thinking that maybe the lack of hair on his head had made it grow everywhere else instead. Iron grey hairs sprouted on the backs of his veiny hands and his eyebrows were like miniature barbed wire entanglements. Hairs curled from his ears and out of his nostrils and the moustache straggling beneath his nose was like the frayed end of a rope. Josh used to dread being kissed by him, thinking how it would feel all nasty and tickly, but he need not have worried. Grandpa Jordan was not the kissing kind. He rarely displayed any affection. He had big yellowy teeth which showed when he laughed, but Josh did not remember him laughing all that much. His tolerance of young children was especially low. He believed that they should be seen and not heard. On every visit Josh and his sister were told to keep quiet and sit still, or told to go and play in the garden, even when it was freezing, even in the middle of winter.

His stuff occupied entire strata in the room. Gran must have bunged everything in here when he died, like Mrs R said, instead of taking it to OXFAM. There was so much Josh almost expected to come across him any minute, dressed in a big hairy suit, liver coloured lips parted to show big tusky teeth . . . Josh shook himself. When he was younger he might have been scared, but not now.

There was nothing to be frightened of here. Not even the rats. Josh discovered traces of rodent activity when he went to investigate the slumped piles of old magazines: *Woman* and *Woman's Own* and more, and newspapers which went back for years and years chewed into nests. Mice, rats, whatever. Rodents didn't bother him.

Josh flipped up the top of a cardboard box to find yet more magazines. Comics from the fifties and sixties. He picked one off the top and recognized the *Eagle*. Dan Dare's square-jawed face, the evil Mekon with his big head, bulgy eyes and puny little limbs. There were Marvel magazines: *Superman, Captain America, The Silver Surfer* and American titles he'd never seen before. These were more interesting than *Woman's Realm*.

13

Josh put the box of magazines to one side. He had quite a collection under his bed at home. Hoarding things must run in the family. His were computer and games mags mostly, but he was interested in unexplained phenomena, so he also had *UFO* and *Alien Encounter*. Mum said they were a waste of money, and was always nagging at him to throw out his back copies, but she didn't understand. There was nothing quite like it on a boring afternoon. It didn't matter how many times you went through them, you always found something that you hadn't read.

He shut the door on the rest of the mess, dragging the box with him onto the landing. Set in the opposite wall was another door. Behind it lay stairs. This was the way up to the attic and the room that had once belonged to his Uncle Patrick. The door was shut and bolted on the outside. Josh bent down. The bolt screeched, stiff with rust. No one had been up there for years and years, that much was obvious. But why was it bolted from the outside? Bolts are meant to keep things out, not in. He worked the creaking metal back and forth. Now that *was* a curious thing.

Dust lay thick as felt on the narrow stairs, but as soon as he got to the top, Josh knew that this was the room for him. It was long and wide, with ceilings sloping down on either side, and skylights. Plus it was almost empty. It contained no freighting of family junk. His footsteps rang out on wooden floorboards, even the carpets had been taken up.

He stood for a moment staring around him. Yellow sunlight spilled down from the skylight, a solid ray thick with glinting motes of dust that his feet had stirred up. The only empty room in a house packed

14

with generations of stuff. There was something lonely, even sad about that. Josh wondered about the reasons, and a little shiver ran through him, but he was a practical person and common sense won over superstition or sentiment. The less stuff in here, the less there was to shift.

The room was bare of everything except for a rickety old chair and table, a bed, a wardrobe, a chest of drawers. Most of the furniture was pretty beaten up. The table had deep scratch marks on the top of it, some of the wooden surfaces looked as if they had been given a good kicking.

These things must have belonged to Uncle Patrick. Josh went over and opened the wardrobe's thin door. Not even a coat hanger, never mind Narnia. Josh carved his name in dust on top of the bureau. He pulled out a drawer, put his hand in, feeling about. Not even lining paper. Nothing left at all of the boy who had once lived up here.

Uncle Patrick. Josh had never seen him. Not even a photograph.

'We didn't go in much for things like that,' his mother had said, vaguely.

The house didn't bristle with family snaps the way that his other gran's did, but Josh had seen a photograph of Mum and Uncle Paul on holiday with Grandma and Grandpa. There had been no sign of Uncle Patrick.

'He died when he was young.'

That was all Josh knew. Up until now that was all he'd really wanted to know.

At some time or other, he'd been told that he'd had another uncle called Patrick, who had died when he was thirteen. To Joshua, that had always felt strange. Uncles were grown up men like Uncle Paul, with houses and cars, who did the garden and mowed lawns. It was not a title he associated with someone as young as thirteen. An uncomfortable thought snagged in his mind. That was the same age as he was now.

It was hot up here. Josh wiped at the sweat collecting under his dark fringe, smearing dirt across his forehead. The room could do with airing. He reached up from the bed positioned directly below the skylight and found that the window could not be opened. It had been sealed up, some time ago by the look of it. Nails showed at different angles, clumsily hammered all round the frame. Why? He picked at the rust flaking from the crooked heads. To keep burglars out? What was the point of doing that? Even a cat couldn't climb up this high.

'Josh! Joshua!' his mother was calling up the stairs. 'Gran's here and she wants to see you. Can you come down, please?'

'Here he is!'

Joshua stood at the end of the bed, reluctant to go any nearer.

'Go on! Say "hello", she's been asking for you!'

Josh doubted that. He still hung back, trying not to show how bad he felt. Mum was smiling at him, trying her best to look hopeful and encouraging. He had been led to believe that Gran was better but one look told him that wasn't true. Mum knew, Mrs Reynolds did, too. Gran was not going to get better, Josh could see it in their eyes.

Josh felt the tears pricking at the back of his nose. She looked so small in the bed, like a big doll, or a little child. Josh did not remember her being as tiny and thin as this. Skin hung in drapes off the bones in her arms, her wrists looked like sticks. She seemed shrunken, changed into something not quite human. Before, at least, her face had held a memory of colour, now her skin was the yellowy grey of old newspaper. Her eyes were closed, sunk in her head, surrounded by wrinkled pouches of flesh. When the lids stirred, Josh stepped back, spooked. He had not expected them to open.

Her mouth worked, trying to say something. It looked collapsed and funny, the upper lip peaked like a tortoise's mouth. Josh had never seen her without her false teeth before. Her dentures hung pink and white like sugar rock in a glass on the bedside table.

'Where am I? Where's the nurse?' The cloudy blue eyes flickered over the area near to the bed.

'You're at home now, Mum.' Her daughter went up to her, taking the monkey paw hand. 'I'm here, and Greta,' Mrs Reynolds stepped forward, 'and look who else?' She indicated sharply with her head for Joshua to come up to the bed.

'Who's that?' The old lady moved her head, trying to see past the two women. 'Is that our Paul?'

'No, mother, it's—'

'It is, isn't it? Where's Patrick?' Tendons stood out like cords in her neck as she tried to struggle up. Tears trickled down her withered cheeks as she asked again. 'Where's my Patrick? Where is he?'

Joanna and Mrs Reynolds looked at each other. They could not have looked more shocked if Gran had

17

sworn. They looked down, mouths ajar, as the old lady's head sank back onto the pillow and began a restless thrashing movement back and forth. Her speech became indistinct as her fingers plucked at the bedclothes, bunching the duvet cover and letting it go.

'The doctor said she might be a little confused . . .'

Mrs Reynolds nodded. 'It's the drugs they get. Same with my sister-in-law. Saying all sorts of things the first few days, then right as rain.'

'Yes. I expect . . .'

The conversation faltered. Josh looked from one face to the other. Mrs Reynolds looked sad and hopeless, as though she was looking back through the years and seeing two young mothers pushing prams in the park together. But his mother looked stunned, eyes wide and tear bright. Her dead brother's name had struck her like a physical blow.

# Chapter 3

'What exactly happened to him? To Uncle Patrick?'

'He died when he was young, you know that. You've been told before, surely?'

'Yes, but no one ever said of what exactly. I mean, was he in an accident or—'

'Natural causes.' She cut in. 'He died of pneumonia.'

'How old was he?'

'Thirteen. Same as you are now.'

'When? When was it?'

'What do you mean, when?' Joanna replied, stalling, playing for time. Not that it was a good idea. Joshua was naturally inquisitive, always had been, and refusing to answer him only sharpened his curiosity. Sensing this, she added, 'A long, long time ago now. 1959.'

'Do people die of it now?'

'Not so much, although they still can. But it was not so easy to cure back then. They didn't have the drugs. Also, he had always been delicate. He suffered with his chest. Every winter he'd be sick with bronchitis for weeks on end. The pneumonia was just too much for him.'

'Has he got like a grave, or anything?'

'Joshua! That's a bit morbid!'

'So? I just want to know.'

'No he hasn't, as a matter of fact.'

'Why not?'

'Grandpa had him cremated and his ashes scattered.'

Josh frowned. 'So there is no memorial? Nowhere you can go?'

'No there isn't. Is that important?'

'It would be to me,' Josh said. 'I'd like people to visit, put flowers. Otherwise it would be rather lonely, don't you think?'

His mother shrugged and turned her face away. She sniffed and reached for a tissue. 'I wouldn't know, Josh.'

Josh was on his feet in an instant, he hadn't meant to upset her.

'I'm sorry, Mum . . .'

'It's OK, Josh,' she took his hand and held it. 'It's not you. I'm worried about Gran. Whether I'll be able to cope. What will happen to her . . .'

Josh said nothing, just stood looking down at the top of her head, noticing the dark and grey hairs mixing together.

'It'll be OK, Mum,' he patted her awkwardly on the back. 'Honest it will.'

'We'll see.' Joanna sniffed again and blew her nose. 'How are you getting on up in the attic? Do you want some help? I can come up if you like. Gran's sleeping and Greta said she'd stay a while.'

'No. I can manage.'

'What about the bed? I could pop up later and give you a hand.'

'It's OK, Mum.' Josh shrugged. 'I've got it sorted.'

*

Josh got a mattress from his mum's old room and manhandled it up the narrow stairs and into the attic. He dumped it on top of the metal-framed twangy springs and wiped his face with his T-shirt. He was sweating all over now, but he was determined to do this by himself. He didn't want Mrs Reynolds thinking he couldn't handle it, that he was dependent on his mother like a little kid. He pulled the bed away from the wall, ready to put the sheets on, and that's when he saw the little door.

It was cut into the painted wooden panelling and led into a crawl-way between the roof and the eaves. Josh wriggled his head and shoulders in, but it was too dark to see anything. He groped his way along, his eyes adjusting to the faint light filtering through the slates. There was something shoved up at the far end. It looked like a box or a case.

Josh worked his way along the gap. He'd grown a lot lately, filling out, getting broader across the shoulders. It was a tight fit. Claustrophobia grabbed at him briefly, squeezing the space around him. He tried to ignore the nagging fear of being trapped forever and used his elbows, knees and feet to pull and push himself until he could reach forward and touch the object.

It was a flat lidded box. He hooked a finger under the edge and pulled it with him, inching backwards into the room again. It was a suitcase. A small leather one. Through the dust he could see the initials P.A.J. stamped in black in the bottom corner. The P could stand for Paul, but the A stood for Alan, Joshua knew, it was his middle name too, so the original owner of this case must have been Patrick Alan Jordan.

Josh left the rest of the cleaning, the bed-making, everything, to concentrate on his find. He sat cross-legged on the floor before it and carefully wiped the top. The catches on either side of the handle were not locked. Josh slid them sideways, triggering the hasps and flipping up the lid.

The first thing he found was a school exercise book with Patrick Alan Jordan written in the box on the cover. There was no school, no form, no subject, just the name. Josh opened the book. What he found was not what he expected. He thought he might find a diary, something like that, instead he discovered numbers, pages and pages of them. He flipped to the front and back again. Maybe it was a maths book, but he had never seen sums like this. There were no pluses, minuses, multiplication or division signs and some of the numbers went on line after line. Who would write down that kind of stuff, just for the fun of it?

Under the book was a pile of comics, or what Josh took to be pages torn from comics. A second glance showed them to be something else entirely. They were copies, but so well, so cunningly done that only the method of colouring and paper quality betrayed their amateur origins. Josh laid them out on the floor in front of him. They really were exceptional, as good as the original artwork in the comics he had found earlier. Josh took out some examples to compare. There was the *Eagle*, replicated exactly, lettering and everything, like a facsimile. More than that. Dan Dare's space ship and the Mekon's strange craft had been subject to special study, drawn from different elevations and angles, internally, externally, like a blueprint. Josh turned over more pages containing painstaking depictions of different types of space craft from sources Joshua failed to recognize.

How old had Patrick been? Thirteen? Josh whistled softly. He was that age and not bad at art, but his work was clumsy, childish by comparison. Whoever did these had been very talented. No one in his class could do stuff like this. The precision in the drawing, the detailed composition: he doubted even his art teacher could match this level of skill.

Josh prised open a small paint box, the little cubes dried and cracked, and felt his admiration deepen. He must have done all this with that. Beneath the paints lay folded sugar paper. Josh opened them out, expecting more astounding art, but this time he was in for a disappointment. Nothing but little white blobs. The sheets crackled as Josh turned them this way and that. It was like someone had been designing their own dot-to-dots, but the dots were not joined up and seemed not to make any recognizable shape. Josh turned back to the other contents. There was not much else: a compass, a pocket knife, an old pair of binoculars.

Josh put everything back as he had found it and sat, arms folded, staring down at the little battered case. These things told him nothing, but he had a feeling that they said everything. They were as expressive and enigmatic as items put inside a time capsule.

He went to shut the lid, but before he did, he fished out the binoculars. Binoculars were the kind of thing that could come in useful. They were old fashioned and heavy, leather grips peeling, the black enamel paint worn off the casing. He aimed them at the window. There was nothing to see up here but sky.

The middle of the night showed Josh some of the case's secrets. He woke suddenly, panic rising, unable at first to recognize this unfamiliar room with its sloping ceiling, or remember the door's exact location. Something else led to his terror. He suddenly remembered the bolt on the door at the bottom of the stairs. What if someone had waited until he lay sleeping and had then crept along and thrown the bolt on him?

He lay back, making himself relax, telling himself not to be silly. He was not a little boy anymore to be afraid of the dark, of being locked in. Anyway, it was not completely dark. Light filtered down from the blindless window. The moon came out from behind a cloud, silvering everything. Josh found that strangely calming: the night sky above shining in on him.

Josh groped for the binoculars by his bed, and then lay back, focusing the lenses, staring out and out. The magnification was relatively low, nowhere near Dad's at home, but even so the whole sky looked completely different. The moon's craters and seas were clear, the stars had different colours and brilliance, you could see far more of them, and they could be seen in 3D, in relation to each other. These binoculars were for looking at the night sky, he suddenly knew. If he had this kind of room, that is what he would do. There was no blind on the window, no curtain, because the previous occupier wanted no barrier between himself and outer space. Why had he nailed the window, then? It was clumsily done, a child's work. Josh put the problem out of his mind, looking through the glass to the sky. He felt a pull of kinship, identity; he was interested in the stars, in astronomy. The sugar paper sheets with the little white blobs? They were star maps, not dot-to-dots. Uncle Patrick had been a star gazer, a sky watcher.

Josh found it hard to sleep after that. He thought about going downstairs to get a glass of milk and maybe a snack. The occasional car went past on the main road, a distant drone, but the house was quiet and still. Josh tried to make no noise as he crept down the stairs, scared to disturb his grandmother, or his mum sleeping across the landing from her. He needn't have bothered. His mother's door was wide open, the bed empty, the room in darkness. Josh padded down the next flight of stairs. The clock in the hall said two o'clock. He paused. Light showed from under the door opposite and Josh could hear the quick choppy shuffle of fingers hitting computer keys. Mum was writing. The words were coming in little bursts as she wrote, paused, and then wrote again.

Josh stood for a moment listening, his ear on the cream panelling. She had written things before, even had them published, but she had not done anything for a long time. Not since she had taken up teaching full-time. She said that the job drained everything creative out of her, leaving her too tired, allowing no place for ideas to grow and form. He wondered what she could be writing now. With so much on her mind, what could she be typing? What was this story that could not wait, that insisted on being told, making her write through the night?

\*

25

Joanna sat in front of her computer oblivious to her son outside the door. She had brought the machine with her partly for Joshua, so he could play his games, and partly for her writing. In the day would be impossible, what with Mother to cope with and Josh as well, but at night when both of them were sleeping, that would be different.

Apart from fleeting visits, she had not spent time in this house since she had left to go to university. Staying here, living here, would stir deep memories. Indeed, the process had already started. Joshua was an intelligent boy with a restless, inquisitive turn of mind. He was already curious, wanting to know more about a family history he had so far accepted, taken for granted. Josh was practical, matter-of-fact, he liked to make sense of the world around him and here he was in the house of invention where nothing is what it seems.

Such a patchwork of falsehoods, stitched together over so many years, embroidered with lies and fabrication. Face to face, it would be difficult to explain. Particularly to Josh who was still blessed with a child's sense of justice, wrong or right, black or white. He deserved to know what the truth was, but it would be easier for her, easier for both of them if she wrote it down.

Even that was a lie. She stared at the screen in front of her. After so many years it became automatic. She was using Joshua as an excuse, she was not doing this for him, she was doing it for herself. She could no longer live with the lies; they were strangling her from the inside, making her as shut down and close-mouthed as her mother. She needed to tell the truth now. All of it. Not just part of it. So why was she writing this? She read through what she had written so far and pressed DELETE.

# Chapter 4

The next morning Josh woke early, but he lay in bed a while, thinking about Uncle Patrick. He had slept here, in the same bed, under the same window, but also with only a little time left to live. Perhaps he was already dead. Josh shivered in spite of the sun shining down on him. Josh had never personally known any one his age die, but it happened, of course it did. Here was proof of it. He sat up. That was scary. For all he knew right now, the very same thing could happen to him.

The sun was pouring through the uncurtained window. The sky above was clear and the day promised heat. Josh was starving. He padded downstairs in T-shirt and boxers in search of breakfast, but there was not exactly a lot on offer. Mum said she would try to get to the supermarket later. Mrs Reynolds had stocked up with tinned goods: salmon, soup, fruit, but there was no cereal and not much bread left. He went upstairs again to dress. He would have to go out to McDonald's. Not that he minded too much; breakfast out would be a novelty.

The centre of town was not far. A couple of hundred yards down the straight main road and then a short cut through the park brought you out near the central precinct. McDonald's was the other side of the main shopping street.

Josh looked around as he queued for his food. The restaurant was fairly full, but not crowded. The clientele consisted of office and shop workers grabbing a quick coffee before work, a couple or two, a family, a few lone adults and groups of teenagers sharing shakes. Josh gave his order, wondering what to do, where to sit. He'd never really been in a place like this on his own, always with someone: parents, sister, mates. He suddenly felt self-conscious.

'Big Breakfast to go, please.'

Having a take-out and eating in the park seemed easier than staying in here. He was too young for the kinds of things adults do to camouflage their aloneness: reading a paper, lighting a cigarette.

The park turned out worse than any restaurant could ever be. Josh had already sat on a bench and unpacked his brown bag before he noticed the skateboarders. Kids about his age, maybe older. They had definitely not been here when he came through first time. They must have just arrived. Whatever. It was too late now for Josh to get up and walk away. They had moved from the custom built area to skate by the paddling pool and the ornamental boating lake, using the bridge, steps and kerbs as ramps, but they had stopped now. His presence had sent out a 'lone kid alert' across the area. They were gathering: boys and girls, clustering together, scoping him out. He thought one of them might be the girl next door, but he didn't want to stare back, so couldn't be sure.

Josh concentrated on his food; sawing away at his sausage meat patty, scooping up his rapidly cooling

29

eggs. He could hear the sound of a lone board being idly rolled back and forth and felt rather than saw their eyes on him. He was not used to this; he was used to being on known turf with his own mates. He had never felt this way in his life before: isolated and lonely, open to hostility, a stranger in a strange place. It was like one of his best games: 'CityScape'. Number two in the 'AlienState' series: *One false move and you're dead meat*. The food had become tasteless, soggy, and about as easy to swallow as the polystyrene tray it came in. Time to go. Screwing up the bag, he threw the rest of his breakfast in the bin.

They watched him walk out of the park. Josh stared straight ahead, hands deep in the pockets of his baggy jeans, trying to look cool, unconcerned, ignoring them.

On the other side of the gates, he had to fight down a powerful temptation to go home, run back to Gran's and the safety of the house. He turned the other way instead, heading back into town. There was a game-shop in the High Street, he had glanced in the window on his way to McDonald's. It looked OK. He would go and check it out. He felt in his back pocket, patting the 'Quiksilver' wallet Maggie had given him for his birthday. For once in his life, he had plenty of money. Mum had given him a tenner just now on top of the wad Dad had slipped him. Bribery because they felt guilty. Being a martyr had some uses. Josh grinned to himself.

He'd been waiting for a new game: 'HomeWorld', number three in the 'AlienState' series. If they had it in, he would buy it. Then he'd hit WH Smith, and ransack the stands for comics and magazines. As he walked along, his smile widened. When he needed cheering up, spending money never failed.

'Did you see anyone?' Joanna asked when he got back.

'Just some kids skateboarding. They were rubbish.' Before the words were out of his mouth, Josh realized his mistake.

'Why don't you take yours down?' she suggested brightly. 'It's in the back of the car, isn't it? Give you something to do.'

'You've got to be joking!' Josh dumped his bag on the kitchen table. 'It'd probably end up in the boating lake and me with it.'

'Oh? Why's that?'

Josh did not bother to reply, just let his pained expression say it for him. Why didn't adults understand anything? You couldn't just go up to a pack of strange kids and expect to join in. That would be impossible. Josh could not imagine anything more humiliating plus they would probably kill you.

'OK,' she tried a different line of attack. 'Why don't you go outside here, the pavements are wide, there's a good slope and not that much traffic—'

'*Mum!*' Josh howled at her stupidity, his expression grading up to thumbscrew agony. 'Skate up and down the road like some sad little eight-year-old? That is *so* . . .'

'All right, all right! I was just trying to think of something for you to do, to stop you from getting bored, that's all! I've got enough problems with Gran without you moping about the place.'

'I'm not moping.' He threw himself into a chair.

'You seem to be doing a pretty good impression.'

'Well, I'm not,' Josh folded his arms. 'Stop getting at me.'

'What's the matter, then?'

Josh gave a look that said: where do I start? But he didn't reply.

'Did something happen?' His mother asked. 'Besides the boys in the park?'

'No,' he picked at a piece of loose Formica. 'Well, yeah.'

'What?'

'I wanted to buy the new "AlienState". You know, it's a computer game. But I didn't have enough money.'

'How much is it?'

He told her.

'What!' His mother recoiled in shock. 'I know they're expensive, but that's ridiculous. What about the ones you brought with you?'

Josh made a face. 'I've played them all millions of times. I've been waiting for this one. Waiting for ages. It's just out. That's why it's so dear.'

'I don't care,' his mother shook her head, she knew what was coming. 'It's a waste of money.'

'I've nearly got enough. I only need another twelve quid. Dad gave me money.'

She shook her head again. 'Well, don't think you're getting the rest off me. Your dad didn't mean you to spend that money all at once, just on one thing. If you do that, then you won't have any left for the rest of your time here.'

'So what?' Josh frowned, and stared back at her, jaw clenched, lower lip jutting out.

'I'm not giving you any more,' his mother sighed, she had to draw the line somewhere. 'And that's final.'

'Thanks, Mum.' Josh picked up his WH Smith bag. 'Thanks a lot.'

'What have you got in there?'

'Magazines.'

'Like what?'

He emptied the bag on the table, knowing the contents would annoy her.

She rose to the bait, fanning the glossy titles, tutting her disapproval.

'*PC and Video Games, X-Factor, UFO Magazine*, Joshua, honestly! I don't understand you sometimes. How much did this lot cost? You've just been complaining you hadn't got enough money!'

'I haven't got enough money for the *game*,' he explained with elaborate patience. 'But I *did* have enough for these.' Josh collected the titles back and put them under his arm, heading for the living room. 'I've got to have something to do.'

'But these are such garbage!'

'That's a matter of opinion. What do you think I'm going to buy? *Scientific American?*'

There was a knock from upstairs. Joanna ran her hands through her hair.

'There's Gran again. Don't mind me. Why don't you just stretch out on the sofa, watching TV and reading rubbish!'

Josh shook his head and looked away. That was so typical. One minute they were stressing in case you had nothing to do, then as soon as you find something, they go mad at you.

The bang from upstairs turned into rhythmic pounding.

'OK, OK,' Josh gave an exaggerated sigh of resignation and dumped the magazines back on the table. 'What do you want me to do?'

'Go and see what she wants and then keep her company while I put the washing on. She won't let me out of the room. I can't get anything done.'

'What's the point? She doesn't even know who I am.'

His mother frowned. 'The point is to help *me*, Joshua.'

Gran seemed fine when he took her a cup of tea, better than yesterday, anyway. Maybe Mrs Reynolds was right and it was the drugs affecting her. She knew who he was for a start and was sitting up in bed with her glasses on and her teeth in. She accepted the tea with thanks and they talked for a while, about Maggie and Dad, school, and this and that, but it was not long before the conversation stalled. Josh thought it was probably his fault. He had never felt really comfortable with her, not like his other grandmother.

Family visits here had remained infrequent and short even after Grandpa died. Gran had never been keen for them to stay. As soon as the family arrived, she seemed to want them to leave. She would wander to the window every now and then, to check if it was raining, or foggy, or snowing, to look for some reason for them to be going. Just like now the nervous chatter would flag and on the way home Mum would remark on the fact that 'Mother likes her own company'.

Josh was racking his brains for more things to say,

but another glance at the bed told him not to bother. In the gap between one remark and the next, Gran was drifting off to sleep. He leaned over to ease off her glasses and disengage the cup threatening to spill from her slackening grip.

The bedside table was covered in bottles of pills and different kinds of medication. The water jug needed filling up. Josh took the teacup downstairs and re-filled the jug. When he returned, Gran was fast asleep. He adjusted her pillows, doing his best to make her comfortable. He thought about sneaking back out again but decided against it. His instructions were to stay with her.

Josh mooched round the room looking at things, wondering whether to go and get his magazines. The tall bureau standing against the far wall held a photo of Mum as a girl and the family group Josh remembered. The silver frames needed polishing. A letter holder spilled correspondence. Josh flicked through. Nothing of interest. Gran's jewellery box. Josh smiled. When he and Maggie were little they would sneak up and sort through the contents, pretending it was treasure.

The other thing they used to do was play with the stuff on the dressing tables and mess with the mirrors. Gran's dressing table had little lace doilies and a green glass tray holding a powder box and compact. Bottles of perfume stood behind in a row. Josh tried one or two – flowery old lady scents. There was a heavy, silver-backed brush and matching hand mirror set next to a group of cut glass bottles with silver tops. He unscrewed one with little brown crystals inside and took a sniff, jerking his head back at the sharp ammonia smell.

The drawers below breathed out silk scarves and lavender. Nothing very interesting here. Josh moved to the other side of the room. His grandfather's dresser was set against the opposite wall. The top held almost nothing at all. A plain flat silver-backed brush, a shaving mug, and a little leather box containing cufflinks and funny little studs. Josh picked up the brush to make a sweep at his own dark hair. Then he noticed a couple of wiry grey hairs still clinging to the discoloured tufts and quickly put it down. He stared at himself in the mirror, pushing back his thick hair, hoping he wouldn't go bald like Grandpa and Uncle Paul. His eyebrows were like black bars above wide grey eyes. His nose was straight, slightly broad at the bridge. He had quite a few freckles, but no spots. He examined his upper lip, turning his head this way and that, trying to see if he was getting a moustache. There used to be a razor in Grandpa's top drawer. The old-fashioned cut-throat kind. He remembered being told not to mess with Grandpa's things, not to touch it. Josh eased open the drawer. Grandpa wasn't here anymore, was he?

The drawer smelt of leather and tobacco, of the old man himself. The boxes of monogrammed handkerchiefs on top looked suspiciously like the ones Josh and Maggie used to give him for Christmas. Underneath them was a pair of pigskin gloves with string backs, an unused birthday present from Mum. The ivory-handled razor was still there in amongst a lifetime collection of odd and broken items: penknives, charred and tarry old pipes, tarnished medals nesting in cotton wool filled matchboxes, a discoloured, dried up Zippo lighter. Josh opened the razor and felt the blade, slightly discoloured but wickedly sharp. He shut it again and began sorting through the rest of the stuff, careful to preserve the haphazard random order. It was like being a spy, like being in MI5. There was something right at the back. Josh reached in and closed his hand on snub lead in a brass casing. A live bullet. Josh had never seen one before. It must have been left over from the war. He rolled it between finger and thumb, feeling the cool smoothness of the metal, before dropping it back into the drawer.

Josh went over to open the window. The day was hot, and the room was stuffy. The window looked out over the long back garden. At the bottom was the greenhouse and shed. The vegetable patch, Grandpa's pride and joy, was long overgrown, but the rest retained some sort of order. There was a kind of patio, with a couple of tubs full of straggly plants that looked in need of a water. The rose beds were choking up with weeds and grass. The wide side borders could do with a good tidying and the lawn wanted cutting. Maybe he could volunteer to do that. He knew how much Gran loved her garden. Out there more than she was indoors, that's what Mum always said. Maybe he ought to help more, like Dad had told him to do. He was just thinking about this, weighing the possibilities, when he saw a movement next door.

Josh hardly dared to breathe. It was the girl. Katherine. In a bikini. She was walking out onto the lawn, carrying a rug under one arm, along with a book, a drink, and suntan lotion.

She spread the rug on the lawn and sat down,

arranging her things around her, applying sun cream. Was this a regular routine? She was pretty tanned, maybe she came out all the time. Every day the sun shone. The gardening project suddenly held considerably more appeal. The trouble was, trellising on their side made the fence too high to see over comfortably. He would have to be on a ladder or climb a tree. Hardly the most natural circumstances. Just doing a bit of pruning? Not the best chat up line of all time.

Still, he would like to talk to her. She was older than him, but not by all that much, and she really was very attractive. Slim, but with a good figure. She was rubbing cream into smooth brown skin on her legs when she stopped and looked round, flicking her hair back from silver-framed sun glasses, her head moving slowly one way and then the other, as if she sensed she was being watched. Josh stepped away from the window, backing up behind the edge of curtain. He did not want her to see him, to think that he was spying.

'Paul? Is that you? Pauly?'

Gran had woken up and was looking over at him, her chin working, lips trembling, her blue eyes unfocused.

'No, Gran. It's Joshua. It's me.'

He went to the bed and leaned into her questing line of vision, hoping to clear up his identity. Maybe she kept getting him mixed up because she didn't have her glasses on and could not see him properly; but going up close did not work, it just made her worse.

'Paul, thank goodness. I've been so worried. Stuck up here. No one tells me anything . . .' her voice faded.

Josh thought she was drifting off again, then her hand shot out and grabbed him. The skin was stretched thin over thick blue veins worming over bones and tendons, the fingers bent, hooked in, like a bird's claw. She held his wrist and would not let go; her grip was surprisingly warm and strong. 'What did you tell them? Your dad's not here. You can tell me.'

'Let go, Gran. You're hurting!'

'No.' The grip tightened. 'Not until you tell me.'

'I don't know what you're talking about!'

'Yes you do! Don't lie to me. What did you say? Where's Patrick? You know, don't you? You know . . .'

'Know what?'

'What's happened with Patrick. Where is he?'

'I really don't know what you're talking about! Please, Gran! Let go!'

Josh was almost shouting and at last her grip slackened. She fell back on the pillows, eyes closed, her fingers resuming their aimless plucking of the fabric. It was as though she was caught in one moment a long time ago. Her lips were moving, as if she was having a conversation with someone, but her voice had dropped to a mumbled whisper, her words inaudible like someone talking in their sleep. Josh stepped back from the bed, breathing hard, heart pumping, sweat breaking out on his upper lip.

'Hello? Anyone there? Only me . . .' Mrs Reynolds' head appeared round the door, hair like a halo of iron candy floss. 'Ah, Josh. How is she?' She looked at him quizzically, her eyes searching his. 'Has she been took bad?'

'No, it's not that,' Josh shook his head, wondering

39

how to explain as Mrs Reynolds could tell by his face that something was the matter. 'She's . . . well, she—'

'Greta? Is that you?' The voice from the bed interrupted him.

'Yes, dear. I'm here,' Mrs Reynolds bustled over. 'Did you want something?'

'The toilet. I need to go . . .'

'Righto. I'll have you there in a jiffy. No need for you to stay, Josh.' Mrs Reynolds smiled her understanding. No wonder the lad had looked discomforted. 'If you can just help me get her into the chair. Sit up, dear, that's it,' she said to Gran. 'Now, you take that side. Lift.'

Josh did as he was told, lifting his grandmother under the arm. Manoeuvring her into the chair was easier than he'd thought; she was so light, hardly weighing anything at all, her limbs wasted to bird thinness.

Josh wheeled the chair to the bathroom door and then leaped up the stairs to the attic.

# Chapter 5

The attic was a handy refuge. Downstairs people found things for him to do. It was safer to stay up here, at least for a while, and find something to keep himself occupied.

He settled cross-legged on the floor and opened the box of comics he'd brought up the day before. He took out a pile of them and began to sort through, separating them carefully into different kinds. The English titles were familiar, and he recognized the American Marvel superheroes, but there were other American sci-fi stories – mostly involving guys in long macs and trilby hats saving the world from little green men in flying saucers. Anything very unusual, he put to one side in a separate pile. They might be collectors' items.

Some of these were unlike anything Joshua had seen before. They dated from the fifties, you could tell by the artwork and typeface. They were all American, the price was in dollars, but they were not comics in the way the other ones were. These were not full of made-up stories. They were more like the UFO magazines Josh had left downstairs, dealing with sightings, encounters, abductions and retrievals, events that supposedly had really happened. Events that Josh knew about, that were famous even now.

There were eye-witness accounts of the Second World War Foo Fighters, glowing balls of light seen by dozens of Allied pilots. A description of the Cascade Mountain Sighting, the one that had given the name 'Flying Saucers' to unidentified craft, written by the actual man himself. There were photographs of Roswell in Arizona where an alien space craft was supposed to have crashed. Someone high up in the US airforce had written about Dreamland – Area 51, the top secret place in the Nevada desert where the US government kept the alien vehicles that had been retrieved. It was all here, along with the first abduction stories.

Josh had not known they had magazines like this back then. Obviously they did, here was the proof of it, but these were American. They would have been unusual. How had kids living in this small English town got hold of them? You would not find these in a local newsy. And who had collected them? Probably Paul, he decided. The box had been in his room, after all.

'Who did the mags belong to?' he asked when he came down for lunch.

'What mags?'

'I found them upstairs. *Eagle*s and sci-fi stuff.'

'Oh those would have belonged to Paul.'

'Are you sure?'

'Pretty sure. There's so much junk up there.' She dished the beans onto the toast. 'Mum's terrible, keeps everything. I must make a start on throwing stuff out.

Bring them down when you've finished and I'll take them to the dump.'

'No way!' Josh looked up from his plate. 'You can't do that, Mum. They're valuable! Even the *Eagles* now. And some of them are rare. Worth a packet.'

'How much?'

'Twenty pounds each, at least. Probably more.'

'Really?' His mum looked impressed. 'You can sell them if you want. Keep the money.'

Josh shook his head. 'No. I don't want to do that.'

'Why not?' his mother smiled. 'I thought you needed money for your game.'

'Oh, and I'm going to find a specialist magazine dealer right there in the High Street, and he's going to shell out, just like that? He'd probably give me 50p, or something.'

'But you said . . .'

'I know, but you have to do it properly, Mum, or they rip you off.' He gave her a pitying look as if she ought to know that. 'Anyway,' he added, 'the reason I don't want to sell them is maybe I'll start my own collection.' He ignored the look that said: 'Not more rubbish'. 'Where did he get them from, anyway?'

'The newsagent's. Where do you think? We were allowed two comics every week. Paul had the *Eagle* and *Knockout*, I had the *Swift* and *Bunty*, then *Girl* . . .'

'What about Patrick?'

'He didn't have one. He was older than us. Two years older than Paul, three years older than me. He might have looked at Paul's *Eagle*, but as a general rule, he didn't go in much for things like that. He was more interested in facts.' She began clearing away the dishes. 'Did you have anything planned for this afternoon?'

Josh shook his head.

'Good. Because I need you to sit with Gran.'

'Oh, hey, I don't know,' Josh said doubtfully. 'She thought I was Uncle Paul again.'

'That was the drugs, and coming out of hospital,' his mother explained. 'She's been confused. She'll soon be back to her old self.'

Josh was far from convinced about that, but it was better not to comment.

'Do I have to?'

'No.' His mother shook her head. 'You don't. But if I have to stay in, supper is Irish stew or tinned salmon. Your choice.'

'OK, OK.' Josh held up his hands up in mock surrender.

It seemed a good point to give in. That supper menu had absolutely no appeal and Gran's room allowed the only clear view of next door's garden. He had tried from everywhere. It was silly to let her old lady ramblings spook him. Whatever else, it looked as if he'd found a sound use for the binoculars.

'It's only for a short while.' His mother was already reaching for her handbag. 'Mrs Reynolds will be in later. Thanks, Josh. You're a good boy. '

# Chapter 6

Joanna was surprised that Josh gave in so easily, she'd been expecting more of a fight. As she started the car it never occurred to her that on such a sunny day, the afternoon would be an excellent time to sunbathe.

Josh crept into the room as quietly as he could. Gran was fast asleep and he did not want to wake her. He moved the big basketweave chair slightly back from the window, adjusted the curtains and aimed the binoculars outwards, hoping that she would be there.

She came out onto the patio area, a book under her arm, and settled on a lounger. Self-absorbed, unconcerned, she began to apply suntan lotion to all the areas of flesh not covered by the brief black bikini. Once or twice she stopped, hand across her shoulder, and turned, eyes peering over dark glasses, half aware of someone watching, alerted by some deep instinct. It was like a game. Josh would pull back from the windows only to resume when the girl settled down, finally satisfied that no one was spying on her.

He kept the glasses trained until his arms ached. Behind him Gran had woken up and was chuntering to herself.

'Just a minute Gran,' Josh said absently, hoping that she would go back to sleep again.

Gran carried on muttering. She didn't seem to be wanting anything, her voice went up and down, following the rhythm of conversation. Josh thought it safe to ignore her, at least for a while, but clouds were coming over, crowding the sun. The girl shivered and began collecting her things. She shot a glance up at his window again, nearly catching him. Josh thought it might be a good time to go and see how Gran was doing.

She was sitting up in bed and appeared to be talking to someone. Most of what she said was mumbled but every now and then would come a wave of coherence, even actual sentences, fragments of remembered talk, words stored for half a lifetime, spilling out anyhow.

'It's not right. It's not right . . .' She paused and seemed to listen to some kind of reply. 'Not my Patrick.'

There was a break and suddenly she looked straight at Josh, her faded blue eyes turning sly, looking from side to side. Then she beckoned him to her and whispered, her voice low and conspiratorial. 'Don't you listen to what your Dad's saying. It's not true. It's not true, you know.'

'What isn't?'

Josh leaned closer, careful to keep out of reach of her fierce bird grip, but her eyes lost their sharp focus. They gazed into the middle distance, to a point behind Joshua, then she shut them fast. Tears squeezed from the corners.

'Not everything. Please! Not everything!' Her voice was full of pleading and anguish. 'Leave me one thing . . . Oh! Oh! Oh!' She broke off and began crying in earnest, sobbing bitterly.

'It's all right, Gran!' Josh took her small hand in his, patting the back of it, trying to comfort her, anything to stop her sobbing like this. 'It's all right. Really it is!'

She did not reply, but the sobbing subsided into muttering and sighing. He patted her hand again, not really knowing what to do or say. He couldn't stand to see her upset this way. Her words made no sense but the tone of voice, the repetition, the worried rhythms, all spoke of some deep disturbance. Last term, they had studied *Macbeth*. Josh was reminded of Lady Macbeth in her sleepwalking scene.

'What is done cannot be undone.'

'Pardon?' Josh turned, astonished to find Mrs Reynolds standing next to him. He had not heard her come in. 'What do you mean?'

'Doesn't matter. All water under the bridge,' Mrs Reynolds sighed. 'She was never a great talker, your Gran. Not until now. Funny that. A marvellous listener, but not much given to confidences.' She touched Gran's cheek, smoothing the grey hair back from her forehead. 'Never mind, love. Never fret.' The faded blue eyes focused for a second, but showed no recognition. 'It has to do with their Patrick.' Mrs Reynolds gazed down then she smiled at Josh. 'You can go. I'll take over now. It's not something you want to be burdening yourself with.'

'Yes, but . . .'

Josh wanted to question her further, but Gran was getting more and more agitated, disarranging her clothes.

'I'll see to her,' Mrs Reynolds said more firmly. 'You get off now, Joshua.'

She shooed Josh out of the door and went back to the bedside. She stood for a moment, glasses misting, looking down at her old friend. Life ebbed away and with it went conscious thought, coherent memory, free will, until all that remained poking up above the surface were great gaunt ribs of guilt.

She took off her glasses and began to polish them on her cardigan. It often happened that way. She had seen it happen with her own mother. The things that she had found out. Greta Reynolds shivered even though the room was hot. Shameful things, rags and bones of family history which even now she didn't like to think about.

'Never mind, Evie,' she stilled the aimlessly roving hands. 'It's too late to worry now, my dear.'

She did what else she could to make her patient comfortable and then went over to the Lloyd Loom chair, turning it to face into the room. Joanna had been noting hopeful signs, saying that her mother was getting better, but Greta Reynolds did not share this optimism. In her opinion it would not be long. This vigil would be one of the last services she would render, among the last times that they would spend together.

Best to keep Josh out of here now. It was not healthy for a boy his age to be involved in sickness and death, and there was no telling what he might hear, what his Gran might come out with next. It would make no sense to him, but he was bound to wonder, was already wondering, and it was not her place to tell him. All families had secrets, she thought as she took out a bit of knitting, but it was her view that skeletons were best left in cupboards. They were more comfortable there, safely locked away from chance discovery. Otherwise there was no telling what harm would be done, what sort of chaos would be unleashed.

# Chapter 7

'Do you think Gran will be all right, Mum? I mean, do you think she'll get better?' Josh asked during supper.

'I don't know, Joshua,' his mother replied. Her true answer lay in the anxious look on her face, the slump of her shoulders, the way her food lay, barely touched, on the table before her.

Josh ate quietly, waiting for her to go on.

'No, I don't,' she said eventually pushing her plate away. 'And I don't know how much longer I can cope, to be honest.'

'What will you do? If you can't . . . cope, I mean.'

His mother shrugged, a gesture of hopelessness. 'She'll have to go into a nursing home, but I'd need Paul to agree.'

'Surely he would – if it's the best thing.'

'It's not as simple as that. Apart from the fact she'd hate it, and I'd feel like I'd abandoned her . . .' his mother paused. 'You have to pay, you see.' She looked around. 'Everything could go: her savings, the house. It's all a question of money. Anyway,' she turned a tired tight smile his way. 'What have you been doing this afternoon?'

'Nothing much,' Josh said through a mouthful of

salad. 'Sat with Gran, like you said, had a chat with Mrs Reynolds, had another look at those comics. Oh, that reminds me.' He put down his fork, ready to pick up the conversation from lunch time. 'There's something I've been wanting to ask you.'

'What?'

'It's about the magazines. Not the British ones, the *Eagle* and *Lion*, but the American titles. I know about the Marvel super hero stuff, *Captain America* and that, it's these other ones.'

'What other ones?'

'Ones I've never seen before called things like *Strange Stories, Astonishing Tales, Weird Science.*'

'What about them?

'Well, I shouldn't think they were available from the average newsagent. I was wondering where they came from, that's all.'

'May I see?'

Josh pushed his plate away, he'd finished anyway, and went to get the titles in question.

'Umm, I remember now.' She gazed down at the lurid covers, the broken jagged lettering promising tales of alien invasion and strange creatures from space. 'These were Paul's. And you are right, they were not readily available. In the fifties, comics were hard to get, even in America.'

'How come? I thought that was the golden age.'

His mother shook her head. 'There was some kind of moral scare, about horror comics making all the kids into juvenile delinquents. The good got banned with the bad, so getting hold of these was a very big deal.'

'So how did Paul get them?'

'Through the brother of his friend Nigel. Now what was his name?' she stopped. 'I just can't think.'

'It doesn't matter,' Josh began to say.

'Yes, it does,' his mother snapped, rather more sharply than she intended. 'I'm sorry.' She smiled an apology. 'It's just not being able to remember things is beginning to bug me. Garth! that's it!'

'What is?'

'The name of Nigel's elder brother. He was doing his National Service in the RAF and he was stationed somewhere near a US Air Force base. He had friends among the US airmen, they used to pass the comics on to him, and he would bring them home for his brother who gave them to Paul. They were all mad about space back then.' Her eyes lost their anxious tired look, softening and widening to focus on a world long past and seldom visited. 'It was the time of the space race. You know, Russia and America? It all started in 1957 with Sputnik . . .'

She sat, eyes closed, humming softly, and then began to sing quietly in a high breathy voice he remembered from long ago lullabies.

'Catch a falling sputnik,
put it in your pocket,
send it to the USA . . .'

'What's that?' Josh smiled.

'A song we used to sing. It started off as a love song but we adapted the words.'

'As you do.' Josh's grin broadened and his mother smiled back. It was the first joke they had shared in ages.

'Space was big news. We used to go out at night to see if we could spot one of the satellites circling the earth. It wasn't science fiction, this was reality. It was exciting to think that man had put something up there for the first time ever, and we felt part of it somehow. Space kind of captured our imaginations and held us in awe.'

'Were you all interested? Patrick, too?'

'Oh, yes. Him particularly. He was the best at spotting satellites. He knew the sky at night. He knew what to look for and where, he knew what didn't belong. He was fascinated by the idea that there were new things in the sky for the first time since time began. He collected things he found in the papers, or in magazines.' Josh would have liked to ask more about that but she had gone on to another fragment of floating memory. 'There was an eclipse, partial, not total. We all watched. It was like a bite out of the side of the sun. You weren't supposed to look straight at it You were supposed to look at an image cast on cardboard, or something. Paul looked through black negatives and dark glasses, I did, too. Patrick just stared at it straight. Dad was that mad with him . . .'

She lapsed into silence, lost somewhere in the past. Thinking that she had finished, Josh was just about to ask something else when she said:

'Another thing I remember is Saturday morning cinema and *Flash Gordon*. We used to play Flash Gordon and the evil Emperor Ming all the way home, I always got to play his daughter.'

'Kind of like Princess Leia in *Star Wars*?'

She laughed. 'Something like that. There were lots of other films,' she counted them off on her fingers,

'*Earth Vs The Flying Saucers, Forbidden Planet, Invasion of The Body Snatchers, The War of The Worlds*. Science fiction was very popular back then. The local flea pit ran special seasons, I think Paul went to every one of them. They used to show the films continually, over and over,' she laughed. 'Paul would sneak in at the back. I think he stayed until he became mixed up with the courting couples and got chucked out.'

'What about Patrick?' Josh asked, curious to know if her other brother had shared this movie obsession.

'Oh, no,' she shook her head. 'Patrick didn't like the cinema. He never went. Paul used to come home and tell him the stories—' She seemed about to say more when her face clouded as if shadowed by a memory she would rather forget. 'The only thing he actually watched was *Quatermass*.'

'*Quatermass?*' Josh frowned. He'd heard of some of the films, but this was new to him.

'A series on TV. *Quatermass and the Pit*. There were a whole lot of *Quatermass* films, but I don't remember the others. Professor Quatermass was a scientist, the kind who is brought in to explain mysteries. In that particular story he was contacted after the discovery of an alien space craft buried deep in the London clay. They found it when they were building a tunnel, an extension to the Underground in a place that was called Hobb's Lane. The thing, the vehicle, had beings, creatures inside it. They had been there for millions of years, lying dormant, waiting . . .' She stopped and her hand went to her mouth, her eyes were very far away. 'We watched it, we all watched it. Dad let us stay up . . .' she paused as though picturing the family scene, everyone grouped round the television. 'How strange. I'd forgotten all about that.'

'And?'

'And nothing. Paul got these off Garth, Nigel's airman brother. Now, I'd better get on.'

She turned away from Joshua dismissing the past, and any mysteries that might lay hidden there, with a decisive shake of the head.

# Chapter 8

The night was hot. Joshua could not sleep. He lay on his bed reading one of the UFO magazines he'd bought in Smith's, flicking over the pages, eyelids drooping, when something caught his attention. It was an illustration in an article about how UFOs could work. The text looked heavy, all engineering and quantum physics, but the picture looked like something he'd seen recently. He read the text around it. This was supposed to be a diagram of one of the alien craft recovered and kept at Area 51. The one they called the 'Sports Model'. Where had he seen it before? He'd read so much weird stuff recently his head was swimming with it.

Josh fished around under the bed and pulled out Uncle Patrick's case. He flipped it open, sorting through the stiff painted sheets until he found the one he was looking for. Different studies showed the craft in cross section and from various elevations. Josh studied the drawing before him and then looked back at the illustration in the UFO magazine. He was impressed again by Patrick's ability. More than impressed, in fact. It was not just artistic talent. He held the sketch at arm's length. The similarity was quite remarkable.

Josh scrambled out of bed, suddenly wide awake, wanting to ask Mum about this right now. It wasn't that late, she might not be in bed yet. Halfway across the landing, he turned back. She did not like to be disturbed when she was writing. The sound of typing drifted up the stairs.

*Joshua has found some things in the attic: comics and magazines. His asking about them turned the conversation to science fiction. The subject interests him, he reads magazines, watches videos, plays games, sees films. I was thinking about how little we had in comparison, a film once a week, black and white television, those comics he found. I was telling him about the things we did. Sometimes he likes to listen, and I like to share with him what parts of my past I can. Our conversation was an object lesson in just how little I can tell him. He asked if Patrick went to see films. I suddenly remembered the one time he did.* Snow White, *family treat. Within two minutes he had to be taken out. My father and the manager had to carry him between them, rigid and screaming, into the foyer. I remember everyone's eyes turning from the screen as we walked up the aisle. I remember Father's fury. Paul trying to defend Patrick, to explain that it was the sudden darkness, all the people, the cartoon itself: a carved house that started singing and whistling. Patrick couldn't cope with it, he didn't understand. Neither did Dad. He thrashed Paul as well.*

*Why couldn't I tell Josh about this? I was about to, but the words became stuck. Too much else, I told myself, far too much to explain; but even as the thought formed in my head, I knew it to be lies. Shame silenced me, as it had then, and has done ever since. Shame of the sort that Dad drummed into us, shame about what happened, shame about Patrick's difference. And, of course, behind the shame lies the guilt.*

*Josh already senses that something is wrong. He's a bright kid, intuitive; he knows when someone's lying to him. How long before he works out exactly what it is? He's tenacious and stubborn. He shares that with Paul, as well as the looks. No wonder mother was mixing them up. Josh will be taller, at a guess, but otherwise he's Paul's spit. Same build, same fresh complexion to go with the dark brown hair; clear grey eyes under thick black eyebrows.*

*They are alike in other ways. Once they get interested in something, they don't let go. Joshua's bound to get curious, especially now with Mother's mind unwinding like spooling tape.*

*He has a right to know, but I'll decide when and how. Before I can do that, I have to tell it to myself. But there are so many secrets. Where do I start?*

*No point in trying to tell it all at once. Let the memories come. One by one.*

#### The Gang:
*First, the Jordan family: Paul – 11, Me – 10, Patrick – 13 Then the others: Nigel, Ian, The twins: WilliamandTrevor. We all lived in the Close.*

#### Nigel Rogers
*11 years old. Paul's best friend at school. A serious-looking boy with a pale face and a thick thatch of black hair. Wire-framed glasses, held together at the bridge by sticking plaster. Small for his age. Paul's protection saved him from being picked on and bullied. Brother, Garth, 19, on National Service with the RAF.*
*Nickname: Specks.*

58

*Interests: geography, maps, space, science fiction.*

*Ian Bryant*
*10 years old. Big for his age, thick curly brown hair, blue eyes, tall, broad-shouldered. Tolerant, good natured, slow to anger. My special friend and favourite. Twins' cousin. Moved away in 1961.*
*Nickname: Bry.*
*Interests: sports – football, rugby, cricket.*

*Twins: William & Trevor James*
*9 years old. Casual members. Lived next-door-but-one from us. Only in the gang because of Ian, he was supposed to keep an eye on them. They were frequently thrown out because they were not considered entirely trustworthy and got on everyone's nerves (Paul's particularly). At a distance they were identical: small, slight, glass-green eyes, pale freckled skin, sandy hair, pudding basin cut, sticking out ears. Almost always inseparable. Constantly getting into trouble at school for playing tricks and pretending to be each other.*
*Nicknames: Dumbo. Radar.*
*Interests: Getting into trouble.*

*Sometimes others would join us, but that was the nucleus. Robert Reynolds used to be a member, but he was fourteen now and considered himself too old to play with us. We went round together. Weekends. After school. Holidays. Free from adult supervision or interference, we roamed the roads, the lanes, the park, the woods, the wasteland. We went on foot and on our bicycles, fanning out from our familiar neighbourhood into unknown territory. Here be dragons. We explored fresh every year, looking for adventure, looking* for the one thing which would focus our summer. Once that thing was found, the whole world would close down until there was nothing else. We lived in two parallel worlds. One real, one not. The imagination can work powerful magic: render the empty house on the corner haunted, turn Paget's Garage into a den of thieves and robbers, whisper of treasure buried in Painter's Wood. Every year we found a different project to fill the holidays.

We spent most of one summer wading in the brook that ran along the end of our gardens. We trailed nets for sticklebacks and minnows, miller's thumbs and stone loaches to stock an old aquarium that Paul had found. Most of the fish did not survive their new glass world. They either died or the cat got them. So we dug a pond. But the water ran away, no matter how hard we worked to fill it. So we made a pool in the brook itself. That was Patrick's idea.

We constructed elaborate dams out of stones, planks, corrugated iron and boulders. One dam was slightly up stream from the other, and both had little sluice gates to regulate the amount of water retained within the barriers. Patrick drew diagrams, which we used to work out what to do. When he was satisfied with our dams, we filled the broad tranquil lake between with fish.

That was in the morning. In the afternoons we went to do other things, but Patrick did not come with us. He did not join in all our games, only the ones which interested him. While we were away, he attended the dams, repairing any tiny damage caused by the constantly tugging water. He would stay there until the light was fading and it was too dark to see anything.

We had rivals, the Marshall Gang, a group of kids who lived up at the other end of the Close. Everywhere from the big conker tree onwards was their territory. The stream ran *along the back of their houses too, and our dam had reduced the flow past their gardens to a trickle. That was enough to spark a war.*

*One afternoon, they swooped. Patrick was alone. They pushed him into the water, kicking and trampling the barricades we had erected, destroying in a few minutes weeks of work. We came back to find the dams destroyed: the limpid water churned and muddy, the intricately placed stones and boulders kicked aside. There was no sign of Patrick. Some of the gang thought that he had done it. He was not the same as other people and they distrusted his strangeness. Paul and I knew better. He would never have done such a thing. He would never destroy anything which interested him.*

*Then I saw him. Further up. He must have run up there to get away from them, but they had him trapped in front of the bridge. He was standing in the stream, bent and hunched over, staring down at the water. The rival gang was ranged around him, some on the bridge, some on the opposite bank. One of them called out a taunt: tentative, testing, accompanied by an outburst of high pitched nervous sniggering. Patrick did not reply, did not move, did not react. The taunting got louder, spiked with confidence, strong in the knowledge that there would be no retaliation. These were little kids, much smaller than Patrick, but he was cowering in front of them, covering his ears, trying to block out their chanting. He could not understand why they were doing this. In the face of their ferocious hostility, he was powerless, like a baited bear, claws and teeth drawn.*

*A stone came over. More experimental than anything, just to see what would happen. We were not supposed to throw stones, it was one of our unwritten rules. The pebble was small and not thrown with any great force. It bounced off*

Patrick's back, splashing harmlessly into the water, but the taboo was broken. Another stone followed, then another, each throw getting stronger. Patrick half rose, turning, trying to twist his body away from them, when a rock, black and jagged, caught him full on the temple. This one had been thrown with some considerable strength. Patrick did not cry out, or make any noise, he just bent over. A thick rope of blood fell into the water. He would be in trouble if it got on his shirt.

Paul let out a howl as soon as he saw what was happening. He leapt on to the bank and hurled himself along the path towards them, the rest of our gang splashing across the stream to cut off their retreat. The rival gang scattered in all directions, less from fear of us than from the enormity of what they had done. They had the advantage of numbers, but Patrick's injury was bad, they could see that. They had gone too far. It was the kind of thing that could bring a squabble to adult notice.

They turned and fled, pursued by Paul and the rest. I went down the bank and waded into the stream to help Patrick. He still had not said a word. He was much taller than me and although he was bent over, I had to reach up to him. I knew not to touch him, but I offered a grey crumpled handkerchief to staunch the bleeding. His breathing was shallow, quickly in and out. He took the hankie, but did not look at me, just continued to stare down at the heavy red drops falling and splashing into the water, blooming in pinkish clouds, swirling beneath the surface.

He did not complain once, not even a wince or a grunt. It was as if he simply did not feel the pain. He walked back with my grubby hankie, now sodden and stained dark red, clamped to his head. Every so often, he would take it away

62

from the wound and examine the blood on it, he seemed fascinated by the colour and stickiness.

He had to have stitches. Mum threw a real fit when she saw him and then went into a major panic because he had to go to hospital. The car was in the garage but she couldn't drive it. Luckily there was a man at Mrs Reynolds' doing a bit of decorating. He took Patrick to Casualty.

She blamed Paul and me, although we were younger, for leading him into danger. Dad's reaction was just the opposite. It was Patrick's own fault for being clumsy and slow, not getting out of the way quick enough, and letting them pick on him in the first place. Him a great lad of thirteen and them just a bunch of little kids!

'Anyway,' he added, shaking his evening paper to emphasize his disgust. 'Since when did Patrick need anyone else to get him into trouble?'

Everything about Patrick annoyed Dad. His difference was a constant irritant. The next day Patrick was back by the stream, a bandage wrapped round his head. He stayed there day after day, on his own, carefully making the dam again. He could not understand that the game had moved on. We didn't mind what he did. Paul and I just accepted him. He was our brother.

Why have I written all this? It is off the point. Maybe it isn't, but I'm still avoiding the central incident. That '59 summer.

Quatermass and the Pit: *Perhaps that was when it started. It could have been. How strange. I've never thought of that, not until I was talking to Josh, explaining the plot. It had simply never occurred to me before. I find that odd. It must have been on TV the winter after the rock fight. I remember sitting between Paul and Patrick to watch it, both sat silent,* focusing on the screen with intense concentration. I was as engrossed as they were; it did not cross my mind to notice that Patrick was watching this differently. He liked the television, but he did not watch in the same way as the rest of us. He absorbed it, much as a video tape does. His favourite programmes were quizzes and game shows: Double Your Money, Take Your Pick. He would sit forward, hands twitching, his lips moving, synchronized to the mouth of the host. He would repeat whole chunks of the compère's patter word for word, even adding in the studio laughter, until Dad roared at him to shut up. He was not like this with Quatermass. He sat still, lips silent, only moving to push his hair out of his eyes. Blue veins beat in his temple where the triangular scar showed livid against the white of his skin.

> 'Catch a falling sputnik,
> put it in your pocket,
> send it to the USA . . .'

We all went out to search the night for the tiny gleam of travelling light new to the sky, but only Patrick searched on the ground. Only he worried that he would have a pocket big enough. He was the only one to ask the postman how many stamps you would need to send a satellite to the USA. He looked every day after he heard the song, just in case.

During the day Mum left him in the library while she went shopping. He would collect all the astronomy books he could find, making notes, filling exercise books with lists, numbers and statistics. He found a pair of binoculars and would lie on his bed watching, sometimes all through the night: mapping the sky, noting the bodies he saw there, tracking their movement to morning.

*Paul's fascination with space had morphed and moved on. He was convinced of the existence of extraterrestrial life and was sure that launching rockets into space amounted to sending out a cosmic invitation.*

*These twin preoccupations dominated the winter, until little else mattered. Patrick and Paul searched the night sky from Patrick's attic window, one looking for satellites, the other for visitors: Little Green Men. We did not call them aliens then. At some point during that time, Paul came up with this theory that they could have been here before, maybe aeons ago, and have been lying dormant, waiting. For what he wouldn't say exactly. He must have got the idea from* Quatermass.

Joanna paused in her typing, stopping to think for a moment before going on.

*I told Josh that Patrick was not interested in fiction, but that is not right, I realize now. Ordinary fiction, yes. He didn't like stories involving people and the relationships between them:* The Famous Five, Just William *were lost on him – he couldn't work out what on earth was going on. But science fiction? Stories about different worlds, space ships, planetary systems – that kind of thing fascinated him. Where he had a problem was distinguishing stories from fact. Paul's theories were based in science fiction, but Patrick didn't know the difference. Paul said it was true so Patrick believed him. After all this time another piece of the puzzle falls into place.*

A noise from upstairs made her hands jerk on the keys. The hairs rose on the back of her neck. A faint thump followed by a high-pitched unearthly scream.

# Chapter 9

It had started with a dream. Gran had been chasing him, shouting and babbling, hands thin and grabbing, pleading and pleading, imploring for help that it was beyond him to give. He ran and ran, but she was gaining, getting nearer, her fingers long and cold, her form vague and indistinct, her voice high and twittering, not speaking in any language he could understand.

That was the beginning, but now he was no longer sure he was dreaming. He couldn't move, although he could *imagine* moving. Can you imagine in dreams? He was just thinking about that when a strong light came on, shining into his eyes. He was no longer in bed. He was lying stretched out on a table. A cold band of what felt like metal held his head while some kind of clips secured his hands and feet. He was fully conscious but unable to move. Waiting. Waiting for somebody, or something.

Only his eyeballs could swivel, straining from side to side, wide and terrified, tracking the grey shadowy figures moving in and out of his range of vision. The configuration of lights changed. A probe was extending from a unit directly above him, the tip blurring as it began to rotate. It gave out a screaming, high-pitched whine like a dentist's drill, getting louder and louder, nearer and nearer, until Josh's own voice rose to join it.

'Josh! Josh! Wake up!'

Josh came to with a jolting start, still unable to move, his body covered in sweat, his sheet wrapped round him like a straightjacket. His mother was there, pushing back his wet hair, wiping his face as she had done when he was little. He looked up into her face and the feeling came back into his limbs and the panic drained out of him.

'Did I shout out? I'm sorry. I . . .'

'Yes you did, but it's OK. If you hadn't have screamed I might not have . . .'

His mother's voice broke off. Josh looked up sharply, shaking off the last remnants of grogginess. Mum was crying.

'What's the matter?'

'It's Gran. She's been taken poorly again. The ambulance is on its way.' She wiped at her face with her fingers. 'Get dressed quickly. You'll have to come to the hospital with me.'

Josh paced around the hospital corridors following the colour coded directional arrows taped to the wide rubber floors. Night lighting cast a subdued glow over everything. At sparsely-manned staff stations, computer consoles shone brightly with blue and white squares and stripes. Barely audible in the background was a low hum as of some great machine, activated to function twenty-four hours a day, three hundred and sixty-five days a year. It reminded him of a space station or some great star ship navigating the heavens;

wide bands of windows made the darkness outside look like the black of deep space.

He had gone in search of a Coke machine, or something to drink, but really he had wanted to get away from the little side room where they had put his grandmother. Josh had not been in, just seen through the window. She looked terrible. Much, much worse than before. She was not moving at all. Her face and cheeks were all sunken in and her limbs were even thinner, tenting the bed clothes at odd angles. There were tubes snaking in and out of her and monitors bleeping all around her. Part of him was wondering why they were bothering. She looked dead to him. Nothing like the Gran he had known.

Josh had wanted to phone Dad, but had been overruled by Joanna. She did not want to alarm him, it was still the middle of the night. There was nothing to tell him. The time to do that was in the morning.

She had phoned her brother instead. Paul had arrived surprisingly quickly. It was a straight run up the M1 from his North London home and all the roads were pretty clear at this time of night. He was with her now. Thick set, dark hair beginning to thin, he looked solid, dependable, square-shaped in a business suit. He had arrived in a shirt and tie as if he intended to leave here for the office in the morning. As soon as she saw him, Joanna ran to him down the corridor, put her head on his shoulder and wept. Uncle Paul put his arms round her, smoothing her hair, calling her Jo. No one else ever did that.

Josh had stood back confused, at a loss what to do. His mother rarely cried, she was famous for keeping everything inside. Josh felt left out, excluded, as brother and sister clung to each other. He never thought she cared that much about Uncle Paul. Josh felt a failure. It should be him to whom she turned for comfort and support, not Uncle Paul. He felt he had let her down in some way.

He found a drinks machine in the foyer. He stood in front of it, wishing Dad was here, half thinking to use the money to call him anyway. Then he thought better of it. Mum might not like it if he went against her decision. Josh fed the money in and then went back, taking the lift this time, re-tracing his route down the corridor, round the corner into the ward.

The curtains on the window of Gran's little room were closed, but the door was open. The light inside was turned way down and there were no red LED displays, no screens showing wavy lines, green on black. The machines were off. They were silent now, there was no noise at all except the sound of his mother weeping. She stood with Uncle Paul at the end of the bed. He was supporting her, his arm round her shoulders. Josh couldn't see Gran. Mum and Uncle Paul were in his way. No one noticed him and he was glad, because then they would not ask him to go in. The young, white-coated doctor murmured something and all three of them left the little side ward and went over to the nurses' station. The doctor stood talking to them, head inclined, long caramel coloured hair tucked behind her ear, out of her eyes. She looked sad and tired at the same time. Uncle Paul nodded his head at something she said. A muscle jumped in his cheek, otherwise his face looked carved out of granite.

Josh hung back, not sure what to do.

'Oh, Josh . . .' his mother voice wavered at the sight of him and turned into a sob.

Josh went to her, putting his arms round her.

'I'm, I'm sorry, Mum.' It was all he could think of to say. Then he turned to Uncle Paul. Gran had been his mother, too. 'I really am.'

'I know, son. I know . . .'

Uncle Paul's voice was low, roughened by the grief he held in. He pulled Josh to him. He had left home in a hurry, without shaving, and his dark stubbled chin grazed Josh's skin. Joanna said nothing, just squeezed her son harder. Josh stood still, one arm around both of them, caught in the centre of their interlinked embrace.

No one spoke on their way home. Uncle Paul drove his big black BMW through the deserted streets; his sister, silent beside him, stared straight ahead. Josh sat in the back, arms folded, head on the window. It would be dawn soon. Josh looked out at the paling sky. When a person dies it seemed that they leave an emptiness behind, a vacuum which sucks the life and colour out of everything, leaving the whole world matt, grey and flat.

Josh went up to his room when they got back. He'd been awake most of the night, but he lay on the bed fully dressed, knowing he wouldn't be able to sleep again. He didn't want to read or do anything. Time and space stretched through the skylight up and away from him and he listened to the world wakening, a milk float whining and stopping, birds beginning to sing.

Josh tried to stay up in his room, but eventually

restlessness drove him out to wander the house. Uncle Paul and his mother were in the kitchen. Josh heard them talking and then the scrape of a bottle cap. From the hall he saw dark amber whisky being poured and caught the rich pungent smell. He was about to go in when his mother said:

'What about Patrick?'

'What about him?'

'Towards the end,' she paused and then went on, her voice quiet, subdued, difficult to hear, forcing Josh to edge near. 'Towards the end Mum was talking a lot—'

'Rambling.' Paul swilled whisky round in his glass. 'Old people do that. She'd had a stroke for God's sake.'

'I know, but every now and then she was quite lucid and what she said made sense. A lot of sense. It was not the kind of stuff she would ordinarily have discussed.'

'Like what?'

There was a pause and then her breath came out in a deep sighing rush. 'She kept going on about Patrick and, you know, what happened that summer . . . There's things we don't know.'

'Like what?'

'I'm not sure but it set me thinking. I mean now, with, with Mum gone and everything . . . Don't you think it's time? I mean, don't you think it all ought to be out in the open?'

'What?' Paul turned on his sister, his voice impatient, edging towards anger. His glass clunked as he put it down on the table. 'Absolutely not! We don't say anything. Not now, not ever. We agreed.'

'Yes, I know, but—'

71

'Patrick's dead, Joanna. After all these years, what would be the point of stirring it all up again? Haven't we got enough on our plates without that? With her gone, it's over. Let sleeping dogs lie, and all that. Here,' Josh heard the scrape of the cap again. 'Have another. I'm sorry I snapped.'

'I shouldn't. I . . .' Josh could hear the catch in his mother's voice, knew she was going to cry.

'Go on. Just one. You're like a coiled spring. It'll help you to unwind. Then you should try and get some sleep. There will be lots to do.'

Josh went back along the hall and padded up to the attic. He could not enter now. They had things to discuss, he told himself, funeral arrangements, adult stuff, better not to interrupt.

Josh lay on his bed going over things in his head. Their muffled conversation crystallized what he knew already. Buried deep in the family history lay a mystery, a secret. It had to do with Uncle Patrick, and it was something Uncle Paul did not want to hear.

# Chapter 10

Josh woke to rain drumming on the window pane above his head. The change in the weather did not make the day cooler. It was hotter, if anything, the atmosphere steamy and oppressive. It was the morning of the funeral. The house was packed out with people sleeping everywhere, like a temporary hostel. His cousins, Barry and John, were in the room below his. Josh had spent most of the day before clearing the junk out ready for them. He could hear the rumble of their voices and occasional bursts of Barry's machine-gun laugh coming up through the floor. Maggie, back from her holiday, was downstairs in the little box room, Mum and Dad in the spare room, Uncle Paul and Aunt Jackie in Gran's old room.

Josh got out of bed and reluctantly put on the formal clothes his dad had brought from home: white shirt, black tie, dark school trousers and his blazer with the badge temporarily removed. The actual ceremony was at ten-thirty, but they all had to be ready well before then. They were the funeral party.

Everyone stood around, drinking coffee, making small talk, glancing at watches, getting more and more jittery and nervous, trying not to get in the way of the caterers who had been brought in to feed the people who would be coming back to the house afterwards. Josh himself could not see the point in that, having a party didn't seem right. He was remarking as much to Maggie when a hush spread through from the front room and up the hall. The cars had arrived, black limousines taking up half the street. In front was the hearse. Josh tried not to look at the coffin under the mound of flowers, tried not to think about Gran being in there, as men in black held umbrellas for them to get into the cars.

At the crematorium, they had to wait for the previous funeral to finish. There were funerals all morning and all afternoon. The order was inside the porch, written up on a white board in blue felt pen '10.30 – E.J.' for Evelyn Jordan.

Fresh organ music started up, acting as a signal to the funeral director's men. Uncle Paul and Josh's dad stepped forward as pall-bearers and the family lined up to follow the coffin into the chapel of rest.

Inside, the place was vaguely like a church, but the trappings were outward, the resemblance superficial. The building was fairly modern and provided a dank concrete casing for temporary groups gathered for hurried ceremonies. Family and friends filed into the flimsy dark wood pews. Josh glanced round surreptitiously, surprised at how many there were. He had no idea that Gran even knew this many people.

The girl next door was sitting with her mother two rows behind where Josh now sat in the front row. She was leaning forward, as if offering some kind of prayer. She looked up suddenly and their eyes met. Josh turned back quickly, aware that he was going red. The front row were the object of everyone's attention.

Rubber-necking around, eyeing girls, was not what he was supposed to be doing at all. He kept his head bowed after that, or stared straight ahead, concentrating on the coffin on its platform of rollers in front of a purple curtained screen. It looked so small. Josh felt tears stinging like pepper in his nose and eyes, it looked so very small and lonely.

Next to him, Maggie fumbled for a tissue and his mum reached out to squeeze his hand as the organ changed from vague background mode and began thundering out a definite tune. The congregation shuffled to their feet, rustling through the books laid out on the little shelves in front of the pews to find the correct order of service.

The local vicar was conducting the ceremony, but Gran was not a church-goer, and it was obvious from his address that he did not know her. 'A good woman, sorely missed, destined for a better place than this, but nevertheless, a sad loss to her friends and family.' Then more rustling and singing, and more intoning from him as cogs engaged and the rollers began to turn. The curtains opened, then closed, and suddenly they were filing out of another door. It was all over.

They came out to sunshine struggling through the clouds. Mum and Paul stood together, shaking people's hands, thanking the congregation for coming, inviting them back to the house. People milled around, greeting each other, speaking to old friends, wandering along to look at the line of flowers piled behind the little stand with Gran's name on it.

Josh went over to join Maggie, who was standing talking to John and Barry.

'Hi, little brother. How are you doing?'

'OK, you know . . .'

'I wonder if they'll do her now or later.' Barry said, looking up at the tall chimney towering above the squat grey building. He was square set, like his father. His black hair fell in a curtain of gelled strands across a broad forehead prone to spots.

'What do you mean?' Maggie frowned.

'Well,' Barry thrust his hands deep in his pockets. 'Some places they cremate straight 'way. Others they stack 'em up, do it at night, so as not to upset the punters.'

'Upset them how?' Josh asked, genuinely puzzled.

'Depends how the wind blows,' Barry cast another glance upwards. 'But you don't want 'em going away choking on the smoke of their dear departed, do you?'

'Ugh,' Maggie wrinkled her nose, 'Barry, that is *so* gross!'

Barry's braying laughing caused heads to turn, including his father's.

'Come on, Baz.' John pulled on his brother's arm. 'Dad's calling us.'

'Kids at school say stuff like that,' Josh said, trying to excuse his cousin's remarks. 'You know, to hide what they really feel.'

'Yeah, I suppose,' Maggie nodded as they watched the two brothers ambling away. 'But I don't think that's the case with Barry. He says things like that because he genuinely is completely insensitive. We've got to be with them for another day, at least,' she sighed. 'Nightmare!'

# Chapter 11

The wake or whatever it was, the party back at the house, was even more of a nightmare. Josh was dragooned into taking round trays of tea, sandwiches, pork pies and sausage rolls. Every time he put an empty one down, someone thrust a full one in his hands and off he went again. The house was full to bursting. He was hot, sweating in his long-sleeved shirt and thick school trousers. He wanted to go upstairs and change into a T-shirt and shorts, get away from all the old ladies ruffling his hair and saying what a lovely lad he was. He wondered why they didn't all go home, but there seemed no chance of that. They were wolfing down slices of fruit cake now and getting stuck into the sherry. Coffee morning ladies, W.I. Quite a few friends of Grandpa's had turned up to pay their respects: old comrades from the war, old colleagues from his work. They were standing round Paul, talking to him about his dad, faces red from drinking whisky.

The rain had stopped and someone had opened the French windows. It looked cool out there, the garden washed clean and glistening. Josh put down his tray and headed outside for a breather.

'Hello there.' Josh turned to see Mrs Reynolds

coming across the lawn towards him. 'Mind if I join you?'

Josh shook his head.

'I couldn't stand it in there another minute. So crowded and noisy!'

'Who are all those people?'

'Search me,' Mrs Reynolds smiled. 'I think most of them only came for the free sherry.' She took Josh's arm and began walking with him round the garden. 'I should be washing up or collecting dishes but I think I'll play truant for a while. Lovely out here, isn't it?'

Josh nodded, the rain had revived the grass and leaves to emerald green, bringing out the jewel-like brilliance of the summer blooms.

'I love a garden after rain, don't you?' Closing her eyes, she inhaled deeply. 'The smell!' She jogged his arm. 'Go on, Joshua. Take a sniff.'

Josh did as he was told, taking in the complex scent of wet earth and grass mixed with the perfume from flowers.

'Honeysuckle, roses, nicotiana, night scented stock,' Mrs Reynolds recited. 'She loved her garden, did your grandmother.'

The old lady's eyes remained closed behind her glasses. Tears were beginning to trickle from the corner of her eyes, channelling through the powder and down the sides of her nose. Josh stood quiet by her side.

'No need to be morbid,' Mrs Reynolds opened her eyes and looked round. 'She'll be out here if I want to find her.'

The old lady sniffed and hunted in her cardigan sleeve for a hanky.

'Here,' Josh reached into his pocket and handed her a big white handkerchief. 'It's OK,' he added, 'I haven't used it, or anything.'

'Why thank you, Josh.' The old lady smiled up at him, unshed tears making her dark eyes sparkle. 'I didn't know boys carried real handkerchiefs anymore. This is very big and snowy.' She shook it out and blew her nose with a surprising flourish.

'Mum gave it to me to take to the funeral. I think it was one of Grandpa's originally.'

'Oh, I see. Still. Very kind. I'll return it washed and ironed.'

They strolled on without talking, both lost in their own thoughts, until Mrs Reynolds said: 'Penny for them.'

'What?'

'What are you thinking?'

'I was just wondering,' Josh started to say.

'About what?'

'About Uncle Patrick.' Josh stopped, surprised. Where did that come from? He hadn't been consciously thinking about him at all.

'What made you think of him?'

Josh shrugged, 'He just came into my head.'

He had been there all the time, Josh realized, he had never gone away. He thought about him when he woke up in the morning, sleeping in the same bed, under the same window. He had been thinking about him at the crematorium, wondering who had been at his funeral. And back here. At the wake. Uncle Patrick was like a gap in their lives, an empty place at the table.

Greta Reynolds looked up at the boy. The thick

thatch of dark hair was pure Paul, but his features were finer, cheek bones higher. The grey eyes, large and serious; sensitive, shrewd and questioning all at the same time, those he got from his mother. She could see little of Patrick in him. But then Patrick didn't favour anybody, he was so different-looking, like a changeling. She stood, arms folded, considering what she should say. Really this was family business. But funerals were often times for air and light to enter dark places. It was wrong that this boy should know nothing of a blood relation. He had the right.

'One thing you have to know about Patrick,' she began. 'He was not like other boys, other children. That was clear right from the start. It was nothing you could see, not at first glance. He was the most beautiful baby, golden curls, big blue eyes, and long, long eyelashes. He grew into a pretty child, kind of elfin looking, but he was strange. My Robert and him were born a few months apart from each other. That's really when I got to know your Gran.' She smiled slightly at the ghosts in her memory. 'We were young mums together.'

Josh sought her eyes, big and dark, their magnification varied through bi-focal lenses.

'How do you mean, strange?' he asked.

'Well,' she walked along, hands clasped. 'Even as a baby he didn't react, didn't smile, didn't laugh, even if you tickled him, it was the most eerie thing. Patrick never looked straight at you either, always to the side, or past you. He didn't walk for a long time. He'd just sit perfectly still. My Robert was up and about and into everything, and what with them being near in age,' she shrugged and plucked off a dead flower head, 'you couldn't help but notice. He wouldn't play with other children, only by himself. I mean, he was no trouble, you would hardly know he was there. That was half the problem. Even when he was quite little, he was fascinated by patterns. He would stare at the same spot for hours. My Robert couldn't understand it. He'd come round to play and there was Patrick lying flat out on the floor. Robert would go over to him, try and get him interested in a toy or something, but Patrick would just ignore him. In the end Robert would come to me, tears flowing. "Mummy, Mummy, why won't Patrick play with me?"

'He didn't talk, either. Not a word until he was more than three. Then he came out with whole sentences, sounding like a little professor. Oh, he was strange, all right.'

'You mean,' Josh struggled to interpret what she was saying, 'he wasn't all there?'

'No,' the old lady shook her head. 'I don't mean that, not exactly. He was bright enough. He learnt to read early, taught himself mainly, and he could write and number, but he wouldn't mix, preferred his own company. It was not so noticeable when he was at home with his mother. The real trouble began when he went to school.'

'What happened?'

'He started at the local primary, my Robert was in the same class as him. Robert took to it like a duck to water but not Patrick. He wouldn't, or couldn't get on with the other children, or the staff for that matter. He wasn't a troublemaker as such, just wouldn't do what they wanted, when they wanted him to do it.

He'd wander into other classes, that kind of thing. In the end they just couldn't cope with him.'

'So what happened then?'

'There was talk of a Special School, but your grandad wouldn't hear of it. He said it was the school's fault for being too soft with him. Your grandad was a proud man and private. He couldn't stand anything that brought attention. He would never admit that there was anything wrong with Patrick, to do that would be to invite pity, acknowledge weakness. The boy was just being wilful, stubborn, doing it on purpose to get attention. What he needed was discipline. He was hard on the boy.' Her hand crept to her mouth at the memory of it. 'Very hard on him. He was disappointed, I suppose, what with Patrick being his firstborn son. Still, that was no excuse . . .' Her voice tailed off slightly, then she went on brightly, 'When Paul came along things got a little better. Paul was more what he had been expecting. Paul was always his favourite. He came to just ignore Patrick. He was very cold towards him, but then Patrick was a difficult child to warm to.'

'How about Gran?'

'She was just the opposite. She wouldn't accept there was anything wrong with him, they were both agreed on that, but she smothered him, protected him, *over* protected him, really. Said he was delicate, highly strung. He suffered with his chest and seemed to have one illness after another. She kept him at home with her.'

'What about the authorities? Weren't there laws about going to school?'

Mrs Reynolds shrugged, 'I don't know. I dare say old Dr Fraser helped her get around that.'

'Didn't the doctor help, in other ways, I mean?' Josh frowned. 'It sounds like he needed, you know, mental treatment.'

Mrs Reynolds smiled. 'Bless you, love, we are talking about a long time ago. People weren't as concerned back then as they are now. Besides, Dr Fraser was very old-fashioned in his methods. He was well past retirement age and no stranger to the bottle. He gave Patrick medicine for his chest, but as for the mind? The only treatment he would prescribe was fresh air and exercise.'

'What did Patrick do if he didn't go to school?'

'He had routines, same thing every day. If anything happened to break them, then there was hell to pay. I used to meet him going off every morning on errands he set for himself, muttering away under his breath, clutching his list and little shopping bag. I'd ask him where he was going and he'd always tell me,' she chuckled, 'in exact detail and then he'd be on his way. Always alone. He had no friends. He lived in a world of his own, really. The only one I ever saw him respond to, who he ever seemed close to, was Paul. Sometimes he went round with him. They had a little gang.'

'What happened to him?' Josh tried to sound natural, but his heart was beating fast, he had asked the question at last.

'Don't you know?'

'Well, yes, in general as it were,' Josh struggled to seem casual, 'but not in specific detail.'

'Well,' Mrs Reynolds paused, still not sure if it was

her place to tell him this. She glanced round the quiet stillness of the garden. A shaft of sunlight, brief and bright, struck through the clouds, picking up raindrops, scattering diamonds of light all around them. What did it matter? It was over. Time to move on.

'Well,' she said again. 'It was a terrible thing at the time. Terrible. A shock, you understand. A shock to every one. No one ever expected—' she broke off, eyes blinking, her lips pursed, her face pinched in a wince of remembered pain. 'I thought your gran would never get over it. She had what I suppose you'd call a breakdown, but your grandad took it worse in his own way. He thought it a shame, a terrible shame to the family. He would never, never speak of it—'

'Why? What happened?' Josh looked at her sharply, and then looked away, trying to rein in his curiosity. He felt his heart beating even harder. What he was hearing now didn't square with what he'd been told before.

'Well—' Mrs Reynolds broke off abruptly. A girl's voice was shouting 'Joshua!' Maggie was coming across the lawn towards them.

'Goodness me! How long have we been out here?' Mrs Reynolds peered back to the house. 'It still looks pretty hectic in there and here's me playing hooky. I ought to be getting back.'

The expression on the boy's face showed that she had been straying into deep water. She turned away from him with some relief and struck off across the wet grass to the kitchen door.

'What are you doing skulking about?' Maggie regarded her younger brother with cool amusement.

'I wasn't skulking. I was talking to Mrs Reynolds.'

'Why?' Maggie grinned. 'Is she the only person who'll talk to you? Oh, what a poor little Josh-u-ah!' She reached down, gripping and shaking his chin, squeezing his cheeks in.

'Get off!' Josh pulled back, he hated that. 'We had things to discuss.'

'What things? She's an old lady!' Maggie shook her head. 'You are one weird kid, you know that?'

'Maybe I am,' Josh scowled at her. 'You better leave me alone then, hadn't you? It might be catching.'

'Please yourself.' Maggie turned on her heel, a fresh downpour was threatening. 'It's just Kath's invited us round to her house. She's having a bit of a party. She asked for you specially.' She added over her shoulder, 'I just came out to tell you.'

Katherine's house had the same layout as Gran's next door, but the walls were all painted white. The woodwork had been stripped and original features restored.

'Mind where you put that,' Katherine said as Barry popped a can, 'I don't want any rings on the furniture.'

It had been raining again, a quick thundery shower, but it had stopped now. Someone had opened the French windows in this house, too. Josh went over and looked out at the dripping greenery.

'Hi.' It was Katherine. 'Do you want a drink, or something?'

'No. It's OK. I'm fine, thanks,' Josh said, turning quickly, nearly bumping into her.

Katherine gave a suit-yourself shrug, and took a swig of her own drink, leaning on the door jamb next to him. She was smaller than Maggie, about the same height as him. Her shiny, tawny, sun-streaked hair swung just above her shoulders. Her greeny-brown hazel eyes were big under brows which seemed permanently raised, making her expression mocking, slightly sarcastic. When she looked at him, the corners of her mouth twitched, giving Josh the disconcerting feeling that she might burst out laughing at any minute.

'Rain's stopped. D'you fancy a wander about?' She smiled now, her teeth showed white against her tanned skin.

'Yeah, sure,' Josh pushed himself off the door. 'I don't mind.'

'Not very good for sunbathing today.' She remarked as they crossed the patio.

'Er, no. Not really.'

'Nice garden, though. Don't you think?'

'Umm, yes.' Josh glanced around, not quite knowing what to say. Flowerbeds, lawn, a couple of trees, not very different from the one next door.

'I thought you were interested in gardens.'

'Not particularly.'

'Oh,' she turned to him. 'That's not the impression I got.' She was looking over his shoulder now, up at Gran's house, to the bedroom on the first floor. 'I thought you were *very* interested. In this garden especially. You spent enough time studying it. So,' she shifted her gaze back to him again, her eyes narrowing to chips of green. 'If not the garden, what were you looking at?'

'Oh.' He felt himself go hot. He pulled at his shirt collar. His skin was beginning to redden. 'Er, nothing, really. Just curiosity.'

86

'About what, exactly? Couldn't be me, by any chance?'

'Oh, no,' he said too fast, shaking his head, looking to the house for help. All he could see was Barry swigging on a can of lager, leering back at him from the kitchen window. 'I wouldn't—'

'Oh wouldn't you?' She grabbed both his arms, pulling him to her. She was surprisingly strong. 'I don't believe you.' She whispered close, her breath warm on his neck. 'And if you ever do it again, you perverted little creep, I'll come round personally and ram those binoculars . . .'

Josh felt his face throb beet red as the last words of her threat rasped into his ear.

'Hey, Josh, way to go,' Barry said when they went back in. 'Reckon you're well in there. Reckon you've pulled, mate.'

Nothing could have been further from the truth. Josh got himself a can of Coke and wandered around, trying to look cool, but the conversation kept playing itself in his head, making him flush bright red. Katherine just ignored him, or went out of her way to humiliate him by suggesting that he might join her little sister's friends who were all hyper and running about screaming, or by pointedly offering him soft drinks.

Afternoon turned to evening and some of her friends came round scenting a party. Then everything got worse. Much worse. He was sure that they were looking at him, laughing at him. One of the boys was tall, good looking with white teeth, tanned skin and a dimple in his chin. He wore baggy clothes and had streaky blond hair parted down the middle. Josh thought he recognized him as one of the skateboarders. He stood drinking beer from a bottle, talking to Katherine. Suddenly he turned, surveying the room with suspicion, asking for Josh to be pointed out, offering to sort him. Josh was seriously worried and about to look for Barry, when the boy grinned. The threat was a joke, which made it all worse.

Eventually he slipped away and went back next door. The caterers were clearing up in the kitchen, loading their van. Most of the people had gone but there were still one or two staying on. He crept past the low rumble of adult voices, praying no one had heard him come in, and went upstairs to the attic. He stripped off his funeral clothes and lay on his bed as the sunset stained the evening sky purple and red. The stereo was on next door, the bass beat thumping through the walls. Shouting and laughter filtered up from the garden. It sounded like they were having a good time, and he was up here like a kid sent to bed early. He wished he was one of them, he wished he was older. He wondered if Katherine was with that boy, or even worse with Barry. He'd been after her all evening.

It wasn't like she thought. She had accused him of spying on her, but it wasn't like that, not really. How could he explain that to her? Dark clouds streaked the sky, drifting like smoke across the window above him. His thoughts drifted with them, and then shifted again to Mrs Reynolds, to what she'd been saying to him before Maggie interrupted. What was it about Patrick that after all these years could cause an old lady to flinch at his memory, make her face pinch white?

88

# Chapter 12

Duty done, everyone departed as quickly as they had come. Dad and Maggie went off very early. Dad had to get to work; Maggie was starting her holiday job. Then Uncle Paul and Aunt Jackie, with John and Barry in the back of the car both nursing hangovers. Pretty soon, there was just Josh and his mum.

'Why can't we go, too?' Josh asked her as they shared breakfast together.

'I can't leave yet. There are Mum's financial affairs, the house, not to mention the contents. There's a lot of sorting out and it's much easier to do while I'm here than from home over the phone.'

'How long have we got to stay?'

'Not long. A week or so.'

'What am I going to do for another week? Please, Mum. Let me go back. Maggie's home now, I'll be OK in the day. I won't get into trouble.'

'Perhaps I want you here with me.' She took his hand. 'Perhaps I need your help and support. Maggie can't do it, Dad can't do it, they'll be at work all day. I'm *asking* you Josh, to be here for me. I'm relying on you.' She looked at him, and he saw the lines of strain round her eyes, the tiredness in her face. 'Besides,' she squeezed his hand, becoming brisk and businesslike again. 'You can help me sort out the house. You'll be good at that, and the quicker we can get it done, the quicker we can *both* go home.' She glanced up at the kitchen clock. 'I've got to go into town. I've got an appointment at the solicitors. Will you be all right here? Or do you want to come with me?'

'I'll stay here, I suppose,' Josh sighed, as different feelings struggled inside him. He wanted to go home very much indeed, but no one had ever relied on him before. To reject such a direct appeal for help would be both selfish and childish.

Josh turned on the computer and stared at the contents of the desktop displayed on the screen. It was curiosity more than anything that made him open the file called: SUMMER.DOC.

## August, 1959

*It was one of those hot summers: the kind that make the record books, the kind that only happen every other decade. The sun rose early and stayed bright in the sky for an impossibly long time, stretching the heat of the day out longer and longer, before dipping to the horizon, huge and red. The landscape crisped and people despaired of their gardens, eventually giving up the unequal struggle with the Mediterranean weather, spending most of their time inside. It was like living in a foreign country. The streets were dusty and deserted. Shopkeepers put yellow cellophane inside their windows to filter the strong sunlight, making the displays browny and green.*

*Fathers went off to work in their shirt sleeves; mothers stayed inside all day, fanning themselves, complaining about the heat. Dogs lay in doorways panting, sides heaving; cats hid in the wilting foliage. The days passed with dreamlike slowness and the rhythm of life became different. People sat out in the garden, or on front steps, far into the evening, going to bed late, rising early. It was a time of strangeness when normal rules did not apply.*

*We went out every day, leaving in the early morning, coming back at meal times, playing the game that had become our summer while all around us the world baked. That year the game was SPACE, fuelled by the Russian and American race to get a man into orbit. Add to that a winter of* Quatermass, *and seasons of films at the local cinema and we were zapping each other with ray guns and fighting off invading aliens. The aliens were really the twins in the green zip-up suits they wore for fancy dress parties and parades. They were supposed to be elves but, for the purposes of the game, their basic outfit had been adapted, augmented by Alice bands fitted with ping pong ball antennae.*

*We built rocket ships in the garden when life on earth was no longer viable. The tree house became an intergalactic battle cruiser. Paul, always our leader, sat at the very top of the tree shouting orders, keeping a running commentary on our progress, boldly taking us into the unknown. The rest of us perched on branches below him, ranged down the tree in strict order of status.*

*Patrick never joined in these games. He only took part when the heat forced us inside to read comics, or spend the afternoon mapping out other worlds, designing bigger and better space craft. He was very good at drawing. His designs made ours look childishly inept. He always drew on his own, completely absorbed in what he was doing, but he showed very little interest in the finished product. No matter how good, he would leave the drawings where he had been working, on the kitchen table, on the floor, casually* discarded. Paul would go round after him, collecting them up, picking them out of the bin.

The Space Game held up well, keeping our interest all through July and well into August, but by the last weeks of the month we were reaching the limits of our inventiveness. The play was becoming repetitive, ragged at the edges. We were becoming jaded, bored even. We needed something to happen.

One night something did.


## THE SIGHTING

It had been a hot day, not clear but hazy and cloudy, humid and sweltering. Mum called us in for tea at about half-past four. She liked to get us fed before Dad came home. He always ate alone and ate different things from us. We might have salad or sandwiches; he always had a cooked dinner, whatever the weather.

Mum said she thought there might be a storm brewing, and the sooner it broke, the better, because we could do with the rain. It did not rain, but that evening the sky was very strange. The clouds were orange and brassy yellow and slung very low.

In the night there was a power cut. I was in bed. The sky was as black as lead. The landing light went off and I heard Dad stumbling about in the bathroom, heard the switch click up and down. He shouted downstairs to Mum, telling her to find the fuse wire, but there were no lights in the streets or any of the other houses. The black-out was general.

I must have gone to sleep then. As a child I was a heavy sleeper. I may have heard a noise like thunder, I may have seen flashes, but I cannot be certain if I am mixing what I was later told with what I remember myself.

The next day, Paul seemed very excited. He bolted his breakfast down and couldn't wait to get out. There was to be a special meeting in The Club Room, which was really the shed at the bottom of the garden. He went off to call the others. I had to get the Blue Book because my job was to write down what happened at every meeting. The Blue Book was really an exercise book he'd nicked from school. He got the idea of writing things down from Scouts. I also had to be sure to bring Patrick with me.

On this particular morning I was not certain that this was going to be so easy. Patrick had good days and bad days, and all the signs were that this could be a very bad day indeed. He was even more withdrawn than usual, rocking in his seat and humming to himself, high pitched and tuneless. He would not eat. He only ever ate Marmite toast anyway, cut into fingers. This morning there was something wrong with the way it had been cut, or the way it was done, or it was too hot, or too cold. Any little changes could really upset him and he was capable of the most terrifying rages, especially if Dad wasn't there, and Dad had already gone to work. He had been much better lately, but I could tell by Mum's face that she was scared he was going back to his old ways.

I showed him the book and told him where I was going. I said that Paul was expecting him and that everyone would be there and he was to come with me. If he didn't want to come, I could not make him. No one could make him do anything, not even Dad. I'd seen Dad hit him hard, really lay about him until he was red in the face and sweating. Patrick's expression never changed at all.

I needn't have worried, Patrick came with me without

any fuss. He always wore formal clothes, like an adult man: tweed jacket and long grey trousers, a white shirt and sleeveless pullover, whatever the weather. He didn't want to look at anything on the way, which was unusual. He liked the garden and had places he needed to visit: ants' nests, spiders' webs. He was particularly interested in insects. He would watch them for hours on end and had developed all sorts of theories about them which he recorded in one of his many notebooks. He thought, for example, that bees talked to each other, moving in the air to signal where the best flowers were. Today he did not stop anywhere, just went straight down the path to the shed. Paul was waiting for us at the door.

'Come in. Quick.'

He pulled us in and put the latch down. The hut smelt of creosote, weed-killer and grass clippings from the lawn-mower shrouded in the corner. Dad's garden tools took up most of the room, ranged against the wall in order of size. At the other end was his work bench, as ordered as an operating theatre. We knew better than to touch anything. Dad would have a fit if he knew that we were even in here.

The others had already arrived. The twins moved up to let us in and we all sat wedged together, except for Paul. He sat on a stool because he was the leader. It was gloomy with the door shut, and pretty uncomfortable but, as Paul said, you couldn't be a real gang without a clubhouse.

'Have you got the book?'

I took the battered exercise book out of my pocket and held it up. The cover was a mess because Paul was always thinking up names and crossing them out: 'Z for Zorro', 'The Black Hand Gang'. We couldn't have a number, like The Secret Seven, because you never knew who was in and who was out.

'Right,' Paul rubbed his hands together. 'The date is?'

'August 25th, 1959,' Ian supplied.

'Write it down,' he said.

I wrote dutifully and added a list of who was present: Paul Jordan, Patrick Jordan, Joanna Jordan, Nigel Rogers, Ian Bryant, William & Trevor James.

'I declare this meeting open,' Paul announced in his 'official' voice, then he leaned forward. 'Did anyone see anything last night?' He asked eagerly and looked round expectantly, waiting for answers. All he got was puzzled head shaking.

'There was a storm,' William ventured. 'Thunder. Lightning.' He threw himself about, hitting his brother. 'Crash. Bang. Bash.'

'Anything else?' Paul asked, ignoring him.

'All the lights went out,' Trevor said, hitting his brother back. 'But that's more what we didn't see. Can't see in the dark, see? Can't see, see?' The two brothers fell about laughing and began to chant 'Can't see, see', 'Can see, see'. Paul scowled for them to stop. Patrick was making strange noises of his own, a high-pitched nasal whine. Suddenly the note formed itself into a shout:

'Shut up! Why don't you listen?'

The effect was instant. Complete silence. A circle of bent heads, all examining the floor for splinters. One of the brothers whispered and the other sniggered, but Patrick was much bigger than them, even seated he towered over them. Neither twin took his eyes off the ground.

'I saw something,' Paul said into the quiet he craved, 'and what's more, Patrick saw it too.'

'Why don't you tell us about it, then?' Ian asked.

'Not you,' William said as Paul began. 'We want Patrick to tell us.'

95

*He nudged his brother and they looked up, grinning from under their sandy fringes. They had identical front teeth, the kind you could open bottles with.*

*'All right then.' Paul turned to his brother. 'Go on, Patrick.'*

*'Mmmm,' Patrick always hummed before speaking. When he was younger he would repeat the question or the last words spoken. He didn't often do this out loud now, he would say it 'under the hum'. 'I saw something in the sky—'*

*'It was the moon, I bet,' William interrupted.*

*'Got to be,' Trevor sniggered, 'because he's a loony.'*

*'Mmmm. No,' Patrick shook his head. 'The moon was not visible at that time. There were clouds, too, and clouds are not good for viewing.' He was looking straight up as if the slatted wooden ceiling was the whole of the night sky above him; staring with such concentrated intensity that even the twins were quiet. 'The clouds stayed cotton wool. Low, low over the house. Then they commenced to glow orange. They became lit up from behind. They were like kettle steam boiling down.' He pressed his hands, fingers spread, towards the ground. 'It was as if something big was hiding behind them. Something very, very big. It had energy lines running under the hull like this.' He moved his hands, thumbs touching and parallel. 'Every so often they would snake and pulse.' He wriggled his long, thin fingers. His linked hands looked like a big white spider. 'Like a web. A web of light. That's what it looked like.'*

*'But what was it, exactly?' someone asked.*

*We waited for him to go on, but he had finished speaking. He just sat there staring straight ahead.*

*'He saw a massive thing in the sky,' Paul added*

impatiently. 'With all lights, and everything, right over our house, didn't you, Patrick?'

Patrick did not confirm or deny. He just continued to stare at the wall.

'But what was it?' William demanded. 'I still don't get it.'

His twin shook his head. 'Me, either.'

'A UFO.' Nigel supplied in a voice awed into quietness.

'What's that when it's at home?' Trevor frowned. It was not a term used much back then.

'An Unidentified Flying Object.' Nigel expanded.

'A Flying Saucer?' William scoffed, his lip curling in disgust. 'Unidentified Flying Bum more like!'

That sent his brother off into hysterical giggles. 'That'd be UFB,' he managed to splutter out. 'How about UFS?'

'How about—' They both rolled about on the floor then, matching the initials to every swear word in their vocabulary, snorting with laughter.

'If you two don't shut up, I'm chucking you out of the gang!' Paul yelled at them. 'And this time I mean it!'

'Yeah, stop messing about,' Ian snarled. 'Or I'll boot you out myself.'

The twins sat up, wiping their eyes, trying to control themselves. They were vulnerable without Ian's protection.

'I still don't reckon there's any such thing,' William muttered, but they agreed to keep quiet.

'Well, that's where you're wrong,' Paul sneered down at them, back in control now. 'We know there are. Tell them Nigel.'

'Yeah. It's true,' Nigel pushed his glasses up his nose. 'My brother told us.'

'How does he know?'

97

'Because he's in the RAF,' Paul cut in. 'That's how.' The mention of the forces silenced the twins.

'He's talked to USAF air crew, and ground staff—'

'US who?' Trevor asked, in jeering ignorance.

'United States Air Force,' Ian replied. 'You idiot.'

'Americans?'

The others nodded.

'Oh,' the twins said together. Anything American had to be given respect.

'Yeah,' Nigel went on, knowing that he'd got them now. 'And they told him that there were such things. Definitely. Garth was actually there, on duty, when a shout went up. Three different radar bases simultaneously detected a UFO invading their air space . . .'

'It's a wonder you two didn't pick it up, then.' Ian pinged the nearest twin on the ear.

'Anyway,' Nigel glared at the interruption and the twins scowled. 'A whole squadron was scrambled and sent up to look for it. When they came back, some of the pilots told Garth, that's my brother, that they had definitely seen it, had it in their scopes and everything, but it just disappeared. He says it happens all the time. In the United States they've even got crashed ones, UFOs, I mean. They keep them in special places out in the desert.'

'Hang on,' William objected. 'If it happens all the time, how come we don't know about it?'

Paul grinned, shaking his head at such naivety. 'Because it's Top Secret! They aren't going to tell everyone, are they? There would be panic. There's a cover-up. Garth said that all air force personnel have been told to keep their mouths shut.'

'I still don't see what one was doing here.'

'It was looking for something,' Paul announced, his eyes glittering, triumphant.

'What exactly?'

'We don't know. But Patrick and me plotted its course.' He drew in the dust on the floor. 'Over us here, then north-west, over the brook, towards Painter's Wood and—'

'Yarndale Common,' Ian supplied. 'Where all that digging is going on.'

'Exactly. That's where it crashed.'

'Crashed!' The effect was instant, all the upturned faces registered astonishment.

'Remember last night's storm?' He stood up and peered out of the dusty window pane. 'Funny storm. No rain. Power blackout before it came.' He turned back to us, arms folded. 'Funny storm, that.'

'We heard it, though. We heard thunder.'

'You heard what you thought was thunder, but it was really a UFO crash.' Paul folded his arms and turned to his older brother. 'We saw it. Didn't we Patrick?'

'What? You saw it crash?'

'Blackouts often prefigure a sighting of this kind,' Patrick spoke before Paul had time to reply. 'A large craft, such as the type we saw, will set up electrical disturbances.' He went on in a singsong chant. 'It is quite possible that this is a mother ship homing in on a distress signal sent into deep space to reach home base from another vehicle forced to land perhaps aeons ago in our time, now reactivated for some reason and primed to guide rescue craft . . .'

'What's he talking about?' one twin whispered.

'Where does he get this stuff?' Ian asked quietly, not wanting to interrupt too obviously.

'Garth's books,' Nigel whispered back. 'They are full—'

'Listen, will you?' Paul rapped out, directing our attention back to Patrick.

'. . . to the exact place.'

'Is that it?'

Patrick remained silent. He swallowed, his prominent Adam's apple bobbing in his throat and stared at the knots in the wood of the wall. For the moment, he had nothing more to say.

'What I think happened, was this.' Paul filled in the gaps Patrick had left. 'The excavations over Yarndale have unearthed something weird, unexplained. That's why the area's blocked off and guarded—'

'That's not what our dad says,' one of the twins pointed out, 'he says it's because what they're doing is dangerous. He says to keep away from it. They're using explosives and all. Perhaps that's what you heard,' he added as the thought occurred to him. 'Perhaps that's what you saw—'

'Of course, they're going to say that, stupid.' Paul cut him off in mid sentence. 'Of course, they're going to come up with some kind of acceptable explanation for what's going on up there, and then say it's dangerous. Just to keep people out.'

'How did you see it, Paul? The UFO and the explosion, or whatever it was?' It was the first time I had spoken. 'Your room faces the wrong way.'

'I went up to Pat's room when I heard him shout. I thought he might . . .' He paused to find the right thing to say. Patrick was epileptic, but that was not to be talked about. 'I went to see if he was all right, that's all. That's when I saw.'

'Did you see it, Jo?' Nigel asked me.

'No. I was asleep.' I shook my head, still staring at Paul.

100

'Truth?' I asked him, knowing that I was speaking for the others.

'Truth,' he replied. 'Anyway, Patrick saw it.'

The rest of us looked at each other. Patrick didn't lie. He didn't know how to. We all knew that.

'So it must be true,' Paul surveyed us. After the near mutiny, he was back in command. 'And we're going to find out.'

'Who is?' Ian asked.

'We are. The gang.'

'Wait a minute,' Nigel looked apprehensive. 'Yarndale Common, that's across Harley's land. He doesn't like trespassers. He's got notices everywhere.'

'And a gun,' William added.

'And dogs.' Trevor didn't like dogs.

'What's the matter? Scared?' Paul looked at us, lip curled, he was still smarting from my challenge. 'I tell you what. I dare you.' Truth, Dare, Promise. Our most sacred ritual. I had invoked it. It was his right to dare us now. 'Who's in?' he asked, spitting in his hand, ready to place it on the floor palm up.

'Wait,' Trevor squinted up at Paul. 'If you dare us, what do you promise?'

'Anything,' Paul grinned. 'You name it.'

The twins looked at each other. 'We want to see the gun. The real one. The one your dad got from the war.'

'Yeah, you're always saying you're going to show it,' William agreed, 'and you never do. And it has to have the bullets in.' He added after a moment's thought. 'Or it won't count.'

Paul had boasted about it enough in the past but, until now, the gun had stayed in Dad's dresser drawer. The gun had gained an almost magical significance. It was real.

It had bullets. Dad had got it off a dead soldier. It had been used to kill people. But there had always been some very good reason Paul couldn't bring it out. Until now. Paul and I looked at each other. Dad would go crazy if he even suspected we'd been in his room, let alone if he thought we'd taken something, especially that. He would punish us severely. I swallowed, mouth suddenly dry at the thought of it, but Paul stared back at the twins, accepting their challenge. Only the tightness of his jaw betrayed any hint of doubt.

'Promise,' he said without any hesitation. 'So who's in?'

'Me. I'm in.'

'Me, too.'

'And us.' The hands piled up on top of his.

Patrick didn't move, he just started to rock. He didn't need to swear.

'What about you, Jo?' Ian asked.

'I guess so.' I put down my book and added my own hand to the top, swearing with the others.

This was no more ridiculous than the haunted house, or the garage used by thieves and robbers, or any of the other adventures that we took from the books we read and applied to our own lives. In fact, this was more believable. Those were based on stories made up by other people. This was true. Paul had sworn it; Patrick believed it and he never lied. I spat in my palm and pressed down on the mound of hands. It was what we did, to swear an oath, to close a deal. None of us knew, as we stared at the bitten and broken nails and tangle of grubby fingers, exactly what deal was being struck and whose fate was being sealed.

# Chapter 13

The chapters did not have numbers. They were written under separate headings. Josh checked the time and started the next one. Mum had a lot of things to do in town so he should be all right for a while.

## OPERATION CRASH SITE

*AUGUST 1959: Friday 28th, the week of the storm.*
*The dare had to be executed together. It was an important part of the ritual, but it caused problems. We couldn't go the same day because Nigel's gran was coming for tea. Wednesday, the twins were going to their Auntie Janet's. Thursday, Ian's mum was taking him shopping for clothes for school. Which meant we had to wait until Friday. Paul called a special meeting. He went to fetch Nigel and the twins. Ian came later, bringing the local paper fresh from his news round.*

*'Nothing!' Paul threw the paper on the floor in disgust.*

*'Hey, watch it!' Ian reached out, smoothing and refolding the sprawling sheets. 'My dad hasn't read that!'*

*'Let's see.'*

*He handed the paper to me.*

*'What do you expect, anyway?' Nigel put in. 'They are*

hardly going to put: "Little Green Men Seen in High Street: Town goes into Massive Panic".'

'I suppose not,' Paul muttered.

'There's this,' I said, pointing to a report of the storm. 'That shows something happened. "storm caused a fire",' I read out, "and damage to crops".'

'Where?'

I read on: ' "A grass fire on Yarndale Common spread to Painter's Wood." Further down it says "Mr P. J. Harley, of Harley's Farm, complained of extensive damage to his barley crop." '

'Umm . . .' Paul sat on his stool, gnawing the side of his thumbnail, worrying at a bit of raw skin. Since the sighting very early on Tuesday morning, the UFO crash site had taken hold of his mind. He didn't talk about it much, not to me, anyway, or to the others in the gang. We were not true believers and he didn't really trust us. Instead he talked to Patrick. Late at night, I heard them up in the attic, having long conversations to which I was not invited. Paul's voice low and measured; Patrick's more high pitched, words coming out in excited bursts. It was as though club membership had focused down to just the two of them.

This growing obsession affected Patrick in other ways. Even Mum noticed. He was quieter, more withdrawn than ever with everyone else, but he followed Paul around like a shadow and, beneath his silence, I sensed a brittle, jittery agitation.

Paul looked up, rubbing blood and spit on his sleeve. 'We've got to get out there. See what's going on. You lot took the dare. Now it's time for action.' He jumped off his stool, jerking his head towards the door. 'We better get going. I'm calling it Operation Crash Site.'

We all stood up, ready to follow.

'Mmmm, is it necessary to take the extra equipment?' Patrick enquired. He always needed exact confirmation. 'The things that we might need if there is a full blown encounter. When the USAF investigated Roswell, they—'

'No,' Paul interrupted to stop Patrick going on. 'We won't need to take any stuff. This is just a recce.'

Patrick clutched the zipped map case and binoculars round his neck, his expression slipping towards anxiety and confusion.

'Just a recce. Just a recce. What about lunch?' he asked. 'We might miss lunch. Perhaps it is not a good idea to go now.' He began walking in tight circles round and round. The twins looked at him and both rolled their eyes to the ceiling. 'I don't like to miss lunch and we could get lost without these.' He patted his maps. 'Then we might never get back. I'm not sure I want to go any more.'

'That's OK,' one of the twins said, and the other sniggered.

Paul gave them a warning look. 'Bringing the maps is a good idea,' he said to Patrick. 'We'll be back by lunch, don't worry.'

There was some discussion as to which way we should go. The stream that ran along the back of our houses flowed down from the general direction of the common, but Ian counselled against that. On his paper round, he'd seen some of the Marshall Gang about.

'Which way then?' We stood about, squinting in the bright sunlight. It was still quite early but already the day was hot.

Paul elected to go by road and led us down the side of the house into the Close. There were few people about as we trooped along the baking pavements in single file. Paul 'on point', which meant at the front, Ian at the back to sweep up stragglers. We reached the end of our street and walked along the wider main road. Soon the pavement gave out and we were walking along the edge of the parched grass verge, our feet sinking into deep dust next to a road where the metalled surface was melting and tar bubbled. Our sandals stuck in black ooze as we crossed to a gap in the hedge opposite.

Yarndale Common, our objective, was quite a long way. We would normally have taken the bikes, except Patrick was coming and he couldn't ride one. Paul thought it would be quicker to go straight, as the crow flies, rather than zigzagging about on recognizable pathways. We followed the stream for a while and then crossed over to a wide area of rough pasture, working our way round one field, then another, keeping to the sides, until we came to a high hawthorn hedge. Paul called a halt and began ranging up and down, trying to find a way through like a terrier dog.

The gap he found was pretty narrow. One by one we went in, wriggling and squeezing down small to avoid the vicious thorns grabbing at our clothes and skin. This was Harley's land. We crouched down at the edge of a half mown barleyfield, peering round to see if he was about. He was rumoured to patrol his farm with his shotgun over his arm and ferocious dogs at his heels looking out for trespassers, especially children.

Paul indicated with a hand that the coast was clear and pointed towards a big oak standing alone near the middle of the field. We followed his lead, still keeping low.

A barbed wire fence had been erected just past the big tree, cutting off the whole top part of the field. It had been put up very recently. Part of Harley's barley crop was still growing behind it. The fence was tall, taller than any of us.

Clusters of barbs, long and sharp, shone in bristling clumps like bunches of miniature scimitars. Paul extended a testing finger and then put it with an 'Ow!' to his mouth. This fence was a formidable obstacle. Whoever had put up the red 'Danger – Keep Out' signs dotted down its length meant business. We could go no further. A wide swathe of rustling barley spread up the slope to Painter's Wood, silhouetted dark against the white of the sky. Yarndale Common lay beyond that, out of sight over the edge of the horizon.

Paul pointed for us to fan out and look for a break, a weak spot in the fence. We went to the right, the twins to the left. They wriggled through a gap in the hedge into the next field. That is where they made their gruesome discovery.

# Chapter 14

The ring on the bell jolted Josh out of the story. He closed the file down quickly. Mum must have forgotten her key.

'Hi, Josh. It's only me.' His mother stood in the porch surrounded by shopping bags.

Josh stepped back to let her in, but she shook her head. 'I just came back to dump this stuff. It's hot today and I don't want it spoiling in the back of the car. Can you put it away for me? I've got to go out again, but here . . .' She took a smaller bag from behind her back and handed it to him.

Josh could tell by the logo that it was from the computer shop. A grin broke out as he opened it up.

'The new "AlienState"!' And after all the fuss she'd made. He leaned over and kissed her on the cheek. 'Thanks Mum!'

'That's OK.' She smiled back at him, happy to have pleased him. 'You've been a good lad and it'll give you something to do while I'm out seeing to Mum's affairs.' She turned away, car keys already in her hand. 'See you later.'

Josh was tempted to leave the shopping on the doorstep. The bag in his hand weighed heavy with promise, but he made himself put it aside while he lugged the groceries in and put them away. He had been waiting a long time for this. Five minutes now wouldn't make much difference.

He had just settled down at the computer screen when the doorbell rang again. He got up reluctantly and went to the door, thinking his mum must have forgotten something, but the silhouette in the glass was definitely not his mother.

'Hi, how'ya doing?' Katherine was leaning against the porch, arms folded.

'All right.' Josh replied warily, remembering the humiliations of yesterday.

'My mum sent me round to collect our cups and saucers. Mind if I come in?'

It didn't really matter if he did or not. She was already halfway down the hall.

'I wanted to apologize, too. I was a bit harsh.' Her eyes flickered to the room he'd just vacated. 'I still haven't forgiven you,' she looked back at him. 'Don't think that. It was still an outrageous thing to do. It's just I shouldn't have had a go at you, not with your gran dying and everything.'

'I'm sorry, too.' Josh managed to mumble, 'I really didn't mean anything by it—'

'OK. Let's forget it. What are you up to, then?' She said, abruptly changing the subject. 'Playing on the computer?'

'I wasn't *playing*,' Josh replied, not wanting to sound like some ten-year-old games freak. He felt himself redden as she surveyed the opened packaging with one eyebrow raised. 'Actually, I was looking through some files.'

109

'Oh yeah? What files?' Her eyebrow quirked higher.

'Something my mother wrote. She's a writer, you know.'

'Really? No kidding. What kind of thing?'

'Oh, er, books and stories, for children, teenagers, that kind of thing.'

'She had any published?'

'Yes, she has, as it happens.'

'Hey! That's brilliant! I didn't know that!' Katherine moved towards the computer. 'She working on one at the moment? Is that what you were looking at?'

'Yes.'

'Let's have a look, then.'

'Hey, no! She doesn't like anyone—'

Too late. Katherine was sitting at the seat he had occupied, typing in commands. 'It's always the first one on the File menu,' she said, as though to herself. 'I'd make a great detective. Here we go. Relax,' she added as the file came up, 'sit down, stop hopping about. If your mum comes back, I can be out of here in a second and we can pretend you were showing me one of your geeky little games.'

She read through in silence at first, thin fingers clicking the mouse to scroll the pages down. It was not long before she began to add her own running commentary to what she was seeing on the screen.

'They could do what they liked back then, eh? Not like now. Stay out all day, come back soaking wet. My mum would have had a fit if I'd done any of that.

'How old are these? When I was that age, my mum acted like most of the adult population were paedophiles and child molesters. I wasn't allowed to the end of the road without a police escort.

110

'This is your mum's family, isn't it?' She went on. 'It reads like a diary, a whatsit,' she snapped her fingers for the word, 'an autobiography. She's Jo, and her brother's Paul – I heard someone call him that yesterday – father to the ghastly Barry.' She laughed. 'Paul obviously fancies himself as a bit of a Julian, but they're not exactly The Famous Five are they? All this swearing and fighting and arguing. Dear me!' She grinned as she read a bit more. 'What about this Patrick character? Sounds a sandwich short of a picnic . . . several short, in fact. Who's he?'

'My uncle.'

'Gosh, sorry. I don't remember him at the funeral.'

Josh shook his head. 'He wasn't there. He's dead.'

'Oh, no. Even worse of me. Foot in mouth disease, that's what my mum says.'

'That's OK.' Josh grinned. 'I don't remember him, or anything. He's supposed to have died when he was thirteen.'

'How do you mean, "supposed to"?' She swung round in her chair. 'Either he did or he didn't. How can there be a "supposed to" about it?'

'Well, I guess he did die, it's just no one seems to know when or how.'

Katherine frowned. 'But they must know.'

'Maybe,' Josh shrugged, 'perhaps they just don't want to tell me about it.'

'That'll be more like it.' Katherine turned back to the screen. 'They never tell you anything. When they do – when they sit you down with "we've got something important to say", watch out because that's when the lies come pouring out.'

Beneath her teasing, bantering tone, Josh detected

111

that her mood had changed. She read to the end in silence.

'What do you think?' he asked when she had finished.

'About what?'

'The event that they describe.'

'What "event"?'

'The possible UFO crash.'

'You don't believe in that stuff, surely? Come on, Joshua!' She sounded like his sister, lip curling at the very idea.

'Well, I'm not prepared to dismiss it. Not entirely,' Josh said defensively. He wasn't going to lie. She couldn't think him more stupid than she did already. 'How much do you know about it, anyway?'

'Not a lot. But . . .' She paused, trying to find the right words to express her impatient contempt. 'It's all rubbish, has to be. I mean, I read a thing the other day that said that millions of Americans believe, actually *believe*, that they have been abducted, never mind seen something. If only a fraction of the stories were true, there would be UFOs all over the place, stacked up like 747s over Heathrow!'

'OK,' Josh conceded. 'A lot of it is rubbish. No one's saying it's all true but if 90 per cent is fiction, that means 10 per cent isn't.' He leaned forward, emphasizing the point with his forefinger. 'Even if 99 per cent of the eye witness accounts were made up, there'd still be that one per cent. Think about it.'

He drew back, aware he was lecturing. He did not want to sound pompous, or even worse, start an argument. He didn't want her to go off in a huff just as they were getting to know each other. Spying on her had been childish, deeply adolescent, he could see that now and felt ashamed of it. The private fantasy figure he had built in his head was very different from the girl sitting here. The real Katherine wasn't just attractive, sexy, someone to fancy; she was nice, funny, good company. Since she'd been here, the time was flying, not dragging minute by minute. He didn't want to be left on his own again. He wanted her to stay.

'I've got some stuff you could look at, about UFOs and that,' he added, trying to sound more off hand and casual. 'That's if you're interested . . .'

Before she could reply, there was a knock at the front door.

'That'll be Mum. She must have forgotten her key again. Quick!'

'I've got it.' Katherine operated the mouse with deft efficiency, clicking their way out of the file and out of trouble. The bell rang again. Josh grabbed the game he had been just about to install.

'I'll open the door.' He handed the CD to Katherine. 'You bung this in.'

'Only me,' Mrs Reynolds came into the hall. 'Is your mum about?'

'Er, no. She's gone into town.' Josh cleared his throat. 'Can I help?'

'Just popped round to see if she needed a hand. There's a lot to go through, you know . . .' She paused when she saw Katherine sitting at the front room table. 'Oh, hello, dear. I didn't see you in there. Playing on the computer, eh?' Katherine nodded, giving her best smile. 'That's nice. Very educational, so they say. Didn't have those in my day, of course.

You are lucky, you young people. Well, I won't disturb you.' She meandered back to the door. 'Tell your mum I'm ready to lend a hand any time. All she has to do is ask.'

'I will, don't worry. 'Bye Mrs Reynolds.' Josh shut the door and went back to Katherine. They both burst out laughing.

'Did you see her face when she saw me?' Katherine grinned up at him. 'Jaw dropped like a stone. "Didn't have those in my day",' she imitated Mrs Reynolds' precise, clipped way of speaking. 'Talk about when dinosaurs roamed. What is this anyway?'

Josh stared at the screen. Katherine was clicking her way through installing the game.

'I haven't had a chance to play it yet. I've only just got it.' He sat down next to her. 'Do you want to have a go?' He was trying to sound casual but his hand trembled ever so slightly as he picked up the Users' Manual.

'OK,' she shrugged. 'I haven't got anything better to do. I'm utterly clueless at things like this, though.' She grinned. 'I have to warn you.'

'That's OK,' Josh smiled back at her. 'There's a few in this series and I've played all of them. They're a bit weird, kind of a cult thing, but not too difficult, once you know what to expect. Here,' he turned his chair towards the screen. 'I'll show you.'

# Chapter 15

Alansom games present:
AlienState 3
HomeWorld

The screen dissolved and re-formed itself.

'Why's it called that?'

'What?'

'AlienState?'

'It's a play on words. "State" meaning place and "state" meaning condition, the state you are in. You're an alien trapped on Earth. Or maybe you are a human trapped in an alien state, on an earth-like planet. It works either way. You could be anywhere. Your backup systems are on the blink. Unreliable, to say the least. Sometimes they don't work at all. Sometimes they feed you misinformation. You have no way of telling what things are, whether they are important, or not important, hazard, or help. You have to work it all out for yourself.'

'But how does it operate? Do you collect points and stuff?'

'No. Not really. It's a quest game. Goal oriented. Part adventure, part strategy. They all are, all the ones in the series. "MotorWay", the first one, is a bit like an arcade-style driving race game, but with extras. You're heading down this highway, all sorts of things coming at you, and you are trapped in a car you can't drive, none of the instruments respond. The other one, "CityScape", you are in this big scary city. At first glance everything seems familiar, but then it's not. They are cool games, not like anything else I've ever played. You have to see things from different perspectives. Interpret signs. Take up totally different points of view. It's the only way to navigate through and survive long enough to find a way back to safety.'

'I still don't understand.'

'Best thing to do is to play it. Shut up now. It's starting.'

The games all began in the same way. A planet, swirling white and blue, showed on the monitor, getting nearer and nearer until it filled the screen. Satellite shots of the planet's face raced up to meet the descending craft, individual features getting bigger and bigger until the screen flashed white, then went dark.

'What's that?' A grid pattern had formed, covering the screen from left to right.

'I don't know. You have to work it out.'

Josh looked at each block carefully, searching for clues. It could be a puzzle, one where you matched up the squares into the correct combination. Or the squares could act like keys, pressing them could do different things. He paused with one hand hovering over the mouse ready to move the cursor up or down or use the ZOOM IN icon.

'It's a window.'

'How do you know?'

'Just do. Just think so.' Katherine took the mouse and moved it to the bottom of the screen. 'It's a door, too. See? There's the handle.'

'Oh, right. Clicking on it should let us in.'

A room opened before them. Dark. Elongated blocks showed in shadowy corners. Josh used navigation arrows to go forward.

The room was replaced. Red, blue, brown and white triangles, squares and rectangles filled the screen, all fitted together in a multi-coloured geometric pattern.

Josh surveyed it carefully. 'It could be some kind of coded touch pad thing allowing you through to the next stage.' He used the ZOOM to examine each area and moved the cursor to manipulate the blocks, move them around, press them in or pull them out. Nothing seemed to work, the screen stayed inert.

'Any ideas?'

Katherine frowned. 'I've seen this pattern before . . .'

'Well, hurry up and think or we'll be back to the beginning.'

'Can you stop it a minute?'

Josh clicked SAVE and then PAUSE on the systems menu and turned to Katherine.

'What is it, then?'

'It's a hall. Like yours.'

'Don't be daft! That'd be a boring beige mat.'

'Underneath that. Come and have a look if you don't believe me.'

Katherine led him out of the room and pulled the carpet back to show floor tiles in exactly the same pattern.

'Hey! Wow!' Josh got down on his knees for a better view. 'How did you know?'

'We've got them next door. One of the reasons Mum bought the house. First thing she did was take up the carpet. Hang on,' Katherine got down on the floor. 'See there? There's a piece chipped off the blue tile.' She was on her feet now. Josh followed her into the dining room. 'It's the same here. There's a bit missing.' She turned round to face him, her eyes bright with discovery. 'The tiles on the screen are the same as the ones in your hall. And I don't mean a bit the same. I mean the same exactly. Take a look for yourself.'

Josh leaned past her, staring into the screen, unable to quite believe what he was seeing. She was absolutely right. The hairs crept on the back of his neck and the pointer jerked as his hand shook. He went back to the hall, just to make sure, crouching right down to the floor. What he was looking at should be impossible, but there it was. He rocked back on his heels, dumbfounded. The corner of the blue tile was missing. He leaned forward, feeling the gap like a missing tooth. The tile was broken in just the same way as the one in the game, right down to the same jagged little edge.

# Chapter 16

The only way to find out what it meant was to play the game. Josh started it up again, gripped with compulsive urgency.

Strange noises came, suddenly very loud, like a dog barking or a distorted human voice. The screen began to go black. A thick column filled the screen, starting at the top, spreading to the bottom . . .

'What's happening?' Katherine asked.

'I don't know, but there's obviously no way out through the front door. Something is filling it up . . .'

'Go back?'

'No. I'll try this.' Josh moved the cursor to the right of the screen and clicked on the navigation arrow which appeared.

'It's working . . . What?' The background colour changed to a deep blue. The image on the screen keeled round so they were facing down the deck of a big racing yacht. Josh tried to manipulate the wheel. It would not budge.

'Try the sails,' Katherine suggested.

Same thing. Nothing. 'If it's a boat or something, you can usually make it move,' Josh said, without taking his eyes off the screen. 'How else do you make these things go?'

'I don't know, but you better think of something quick.' The game was getting to Katherine, she was beginning to sound panicky. 'The howling's getting worse! The shadow thing is coming!'

'Only one thing left to do.'

A memory tugged at his consciousness, unlocking the puzzle. He took the cursor up to the prow and pointed over the side.

'What are you doing? We'll be in the sea!'

'I don't think so. It's not real,' Josh explained. 'None of the instruments respond. It's a model.'

Sure enough, the camera angle changed, shifting the point of view. Suddenly they were looking at a replica sitting on a shelf.

'Phew! Thank goodness for that!' Katherine's relief was heartfelt.

'Calm down,' Josh instructed. 'If you stress too much you'll lose it.'

'Oh, no!' Katherine screamed. 'The shadow's eating up the floor!'

'Hey! What did I just say?' Josh said with a slight shake of his head, but it was his turn to jump as he glanced up and saw a dark shape crossing the hallway, stopping at the door.

'Mum! I didn't hear you come in.' Josh got up quickly and came out to her.

The girl from next door smiled up from the computer screen.

'Katherine's here,' Josh offered by way of explanation.

'So I see. I hate to break things up but I need to use

this room.' Joanna Parker smiled back at them, trying to disguise the surprise she was feeling.

'That's OK. We can go round Kath's house. That's if you don't mind . . .'

'Not at all.'

Joanna made herself a cup of tea as they packed the game away and left the house. What was going on here? It must all have happened while she was out. Katherine seemed a nice enough girl, and she was very pretty, but what on earth could she possibly see in Josh? She was older than him for a start. Josh had developed a bit of a crush, that much was obvious. She'd seen the way he looked at her, yesterday at the funeral, and afterwards. Her son was not a child anymore, she knew that, but still the realization had come as a shock. He was bound to start becoming interested in girls, and he was a good-looking boy, they were going to be interested back.

She took her tea back into the dining room and looked at the blank screen. In the quiet of the house, the pain she felt was almost physical. She told herself it was concern, a hope that this girl wouldn't hurt him, but it felt like something else. It felt like jealousy. She hadn't experienced this when Maggie started having boyfriends. She'd felt a kind of pride. Perhaps it was different with boys. Josh was growing up. It was bound to happen some time, she told herself. It was good he'd found someone. Playing games on your own was no fun. She turned on the computer.

The insistent ringing turned into the tap of metal on glass. Joanna looked up from the computer to see

Mrs Reynolds rapping on the window. Reluctantly she closed her story down and went to the door.

'Only me. I've mislaid my key. I called earlier, did Joshua tell you?'

Joanna shook her head. She'd been writing for a long time and sometimes it was like waking from sleep and she found it hard to speak.

'Well, I just popped round to see if you needed a hand. I know what it was like after Herbert died, and my sister. So much to do. Have you been to the solicitor?'

Joanna nodded.

'Paperwork sorted out? Solicitors are usually keen as mustard on getting all that in order.'

Joanna bit her lip. The old lady's question hit a nerve. She'd been putting it off. He'd asked her on the day before the funeral, and again this morning.

'Well, I'd advise you to get cracking on it as quick as possible. The funeral's over now, no point in dragging it out. The sooner you get everything in order here, the sooner you can get home and get on with your own life.' The old lady smiled and put her hand on the younger woman's arm. 'You don't want to linger here, my dear. It's not good for you, or young Joshua. Too much death. Too many memories. Now, do you know where to look? Sometimes documents are hard to track down . . .'

'Oh, yes. They'll be in Dad's room, in the desk.'

'Well, I'd check if I was you. Had the devil of a job with my sister. Couldn't find the deeds of the house. Found them in a chocolate box at the back of her wardrobe when I was chucking out. Well, can't stop. I'm expecting some of the W.I. That's why I came round, really. To see if you want a hand with your mum's clothes. We're having a Bring and Buy on Saturday.'

'That's a good idea. Thanks. I'll bag them up ready.'

The heavy cream-painted door was not locked, just unwilling to open. It stuck at the bottom as Joanna Parker pushed her way into the small, cramped room off the hall, next to the front door. In other houses the space was described as 'the lobby' and used as a downstairs cloakroom. Her father had made it into his study. Joanna gave one more shove and the door juddered far enough ajar for her to squeeze inside.

The fingers of one hand could count the times that she had been in here. To hand over her music and exam certificates, to be told her 11-plus result. Each time she entered, she had been nervous. There was no one here now to cause this fear, but memory was enough to raise the hairs on her arms and make the butterflies flutter and stir.

The room smelt very faintly of him. Joanna sniffed: the rich mix of leather, tweed, pipe tobacco, the thin taint of acrid smoke. A row of tarry charcoal-bowled specimens still stood to attention in a pipe-rack Paul had made in Woodwork. Joanna remembered when it had been given as a Christmas present: the lengthy unwrapping, the careful folding of the paper so it could be used the following year. Then came the painstaking examination, the criticism of the clumsy construction, how the dovetail joints were cut. It was never Dad's way to hand out praise, but he had used it. He had taken it to his room, slotting in his favourites, and here it was still, holding up pipes.

Shelves, a yard long, a foot wide, ranged up the walls. These were empty now, the dust lay thick as felt, but they had held her father's model boat collection. Sailing yachts, fishing smacks and motor cruisers with little petrol engines had once had pride of place here. On his death they had been donated to the Model Boat Club. None of his family had ever been allowed to touch even one of them.

Every Sunday morning, he would go down to the lake in the park, with his chosen boat tucked under one arm. He always wore the same outfit. In the winter, overcoat and trilby hat; in the summer, Panama and linen jacket. Sailing the boats was a strictly solitary adult activity. None of his children, or grandchildren for that matter, ever went with him. He would spend from ten o'clock until twelve thus engaged and then he would return, expecting dinner on the table at one. He was like that in everything. You really could set your watch by him.

A big oak rolltop desk took up half the room. Joanna went over to it and sat in the captain's chair facing the ribbed panels and brass-handled drawers. A short gold topped cane, a swagger stick left over from his days in the army, lay along the top. A bottle of Quink stood next to it, the ink level tide marked down to a navy blue residue.

The solicitor would need the deeds of the house, insurance certificates, bank and building society details, all kinds of things like that. Joanna reached forward. The lid rattled back. Papers and documents began to spill out, stiff folds still holding the shapes of the envelopes.

Joanna pulled back in distaste, reluctant to touch

any of it. She would have to really make herself plough through this lot. Dad never threw anything away and everything got put in here, from birth certificates to gas bills. On his death, Mum had clearly not bothered to sort it out; by the look of it, she had just followed suit. Going through it all could take most of the evening. It was a good job Josh had gone next door. There was no knowing what might come to light and she did not want to be interrupted.

She cleared out the top part of the desk, carrying the contents in armfuls and putting them on the dining room table. She began sorting the dross from the useful, discarding the rubbish, keeping only important documents: bank account details, building society books, stocks and shares, insurance policies. The certificates that mark our passage through life: birth, marriage, death. She flattened out the long, folded documents. Each was numbered, dated, stamped and witnessed, details of place, name and status entered in neat copperplate writing, the ink now fading into the red and green watermarked paper. Joanna had added her mother's death certificate to the top, black ink barely dry on the registrar's neat italic. Then she stood back, face perplexed, fingers drumming on the table. Something was missing.

Finally she went back to her father's room and sat in his chair. It was almost too dark to see but she did not put on the light. Where was Patrick's death certificate? The solicitor needed to see it. Something odd about the will. His death certificate should have been in the desk but it was not there. She had been through everything twice, even turned out the bin bags. It might be in one of these drawers. She opened one and encountered a fresh paper storm. She shut it again and left the room. She really was too tired now. That task could wait until morning.

Josh came back late. They had been playing the game all afternoon and most of the evening. Katherine had got into it in a surprising way. She had proved a natural: inventive, resourceful, quick-witted, better than him at getting inside the strange alien mindset the game required.

In his experience, strategy and adventures did not always appeal to girls. The games were too obsessive, took up too much time, required concentrated attention to detail not wholly relevant to real-life situations. Katherine had not reacted in that way at all. She had become enthralled, recording every scrap of evidence, plotting a path, logging their way through. There was no map with the game so she was making her own, complete with names: Hall of Mosaics, Boat Room, Sky Loft, Crawl Through, Ladder Stairs.

He would probably still be round at her house now if her mum hadn't called time and thrown him out.

The layout was basically a house and at this point the game had two objectives:

a) Escape to the outside world (not that you knew anything about that. All the windows were black). There was only one viable exit and so far they had failed to find it.

b) Escape pursuers. Hostile forces roamed the house. Shadowman had been joined by others: Howlers and Two Black Figures (Katherine's term again, threats were never named in any of these games).

Josh opened the front door and stepped into the hall. Despite the flattening effect of the computer graphics, the house *was* like the one he was in now. Very like, in fact. So alike that Katherine thought that they were identical, citing the chipped floor tile as proof. Josh wanted to dismiss this as fanciful. How could it possibly be the same? The tiles were probably a common design, and it was not unheard of for them to get chipped and damaged, especially the ones by the door.

From the dining room came the hurried tap tap of his mother's typing. Josh stood frowning, deep in thought, then he flipped back the mat to take another look. The tiles had not changed since he had been away. The blue one was chipped just the same, just like the one in the game.

'Are you hungry?' His mother's voice came through the door, pulling him back to reality.

'No, I'm OK, thanks. Kath's mum gave me pizza.'

''Night, then.'

''Night, Mum.'

He mounted the stairs and got ready for bed, trying to stop it all spinning round in his head. He needed to sleep, not lie awake going over every move again. That was the thing about these games. The world they created went on gathering significance, growing in meaning, long after the screen was turned off. Until, for some people, the game was more real than the actual world around them, not to mention more exciting. It all added to the fascination. Josh lay in bed, unable to sleep, staring up at the stars. His fingers itched, twitching for the keyboard. He had played plenty of games. The really great ones had filled his mind, his days, his nights, for weeks, months at a time; but he had never played one set in his own house. The actual place where he was living.

# Chapter 17

Katherine said she'd either phone or come round. So far she had done neither. Josh had turned on the computer and sat in front of it, staring at the screen saver, plagued by doubts. She'd just been stringing him along yesterday. That was almost certain. She wasn't really interested, how could she be? Computer games were little kid things. OK if there was nothing else to do. One of her friends had probably called with an all-round better prospect. Probably the skater boy from the party, the one with the floppy hair and white teeth and the dimple in his chin. He had called her up this morning to go somewhere and do something exciting.

Josh was not sure what they would do, or where that boy would take her, but it was bound to be better than coming round here to spend time with him.

He could play the game himself, except he'd left the CD at her house. He could go round there, but he did not want to do that. He clicked on SUMMER.DOC. Mum had gone back to see the solicitor so he would be quite safe, at least for a while.

*We went to the right, the twins to the left. They wriggled* through a gap in the hedge into the next field. That is where they made their gruesome discovery.

One of the twins reappeared on hands and knees, face white, yelling for help. The next field was rough pasture, hummocky and patched with gorse and bracken. The shining steel fence crossed here, too. Sheep grazed right up next to it. Some of their wool had snagged in the wire. It hung down in wispy dirty yellow strands.

One of the twins was there to meet us, the other was on all fours like a dog, throwing up, body heaving. We left him, juddering and racked, and went to see what they had found.

The smell alerted us: sweetish, sickening, something dead and rotting. The air was heavy with the drone of flies; an undulating sheet, shimmering metallic blue and green in the summer heat.

'What is it?' Ian asked, his face wrinkling up in disgust.

'A sheep.' Paul replied, pointing to the patches of white wool between the black, blood-encrusted wounds. It lay in a dip in the field, half under a stunted thorn bush.

'What happened to it?' Nigel asked, using his hands as a face mask.

'Search me.' Paul shook his head.

We stayed, unable to break away from the terrible reality of death. This was the first dead thing I had seen. I stared on as fascinated and appalled as the rest of them. The sheep lay with its head thrown back. The muzzle was torn away to expose the teeth. Black rimmed sockets opened where the eye and ear should have been; the neck, stripped down to white vertebrae, lay bent in a supple curve of ivory. What I had first taken to be curling fleece turned out to be a creamy mass of maggots, moving and pulsating along the curve of its flank.

130

'Oh, no! Oh, yuk!' Nigel kept saying. 'That is disgusting.'

'Come on,' Paul began, then he stopped. 'Patrick!' He grabbed his brother's arm. 'Get away from it! For God's sake, don't touch it!'

Patrick was kneeling, reaching curious fingers towards the carcass.

'Why not?' He looked up at his brother, shaking him off.

'Because it's dirty. You'll get diseases.'

Patrick sat down, oblivious of the smell and everything else.

'It's interesting. I want to stay here. I want to watch.' He stared back at us. Mouth set in a thin line, blue eyes blank, high forehead arrowed with stubborn frown lines. Paul and I looked at each other.

'He's mad!' William whispered with a shudder. 'Wanting to touch that, that thing!' His voice rose clear, shouting his contempt into the still air. 'He's daft, barmy, cracked in the head!'

'What did you say?' Paul lunged at William, but both twins skipped off to a safe distance and began to chant: 'Cracky, barmy, Patrick is a dafty!'

Paul leapt after them, but I dropped onto one knee beside Patrick, screening out the twins' provocation and the chase that had begun.

'You can't stay here, Patrick.'

'Why not?' His voice had risen now, shrill and quarrelsome.

'Because our journey isn't over yet.' I touched the binoculars and map case. 'We need you to navigate.'

'Oh, yes. I had forgotten about that.' He stood up then, dusting his hands. 'Can I come back after?'

'Maybe. We'll have to see,' Paul replied, walking back. The twins, looking suitably cowed, were lurking at a safe

131

distance. He beckoned us to follow him to the five bar gate which separated this field from the next. 'Come on. Let's go.'

Paul jumped off onto the other side. This field contained barley, like the first. The new barbed wire fence crossed here as well, cutting through the tall grain, looping up towards the next hedge.

'Damn,' Paul looked up towards Painter's Wood. 'What are we going to do?'

'Shh!' Ian held his finger to his lips. 'Listen.'

We all froze, picking up the deep background hum and grind of heavy machinery. With this came another sound: the thud, thud of rotor blades chopping the air.

A helicopter!

A rare sight.

One to be prized.

The twins hopped away from the fence, searching the skies, wanting to be the first one to see it.

'There it is! There!' Trevor was shading his eyes, pointing straight up in the air.

'That's a bird, stupid! There it is!' William turned and turned before settling, arm extended, facing up the hill, pointing to the ragged black fringe of Painter's Wood.

The helicopter rose from behind the trees like a monstrous insect. Rocking in the air, it seemed to look down at us, its Perspex windscreens like huge bulging compound eyes. Its rattle and thrum beat around us and Patrick covered his ears with his hands, pressing them into the sides of his head, his face contorting in agony. He had always hated loud noises. Now his high pitched screaming joined the heavy thud of the rotor arms as he whirled around and around, trying to get away from the sound.

132

'Get down! Get down!' Paul shouted, pulling him to the ground.

We flattened ourselves, cowering into the barley stands. The stems whipped wildly, threshed by the savage down draft, as the helicopter rose over the wood and swooped down towards us. It hovered for a moment and we all held our breath, then it was gone, veering off and away like some great dragonfly.

'It's all right now.' Paul called. 'All clear.' He stood up and looked round. 'Everyone OK?'

We nodded, sitting up, dusty and shaken.

'What was a helicopter doing here?' Paul asked, looking up at the sky, not expecting any reply. His gaze changed to follow the line of exclusion signs spread along the shining new fence. 'What's going on past here?' He looked up the hill towards the dark band of woodland and then went over and touched the wire, more cautiously this time. 'Is this to keep us out, or something else in?' He looked at his watch. 'Reconnaissance Trip: Operation Crash Site: halted 11:40 hours GMT. Operation Crash Site,' he repeated to the questioning looks turned towards him. 'That's what I'm going to call it. Because this is a crash site, got to be.' He gestured behind him. 'This will call for further investigation and more detailed preparation. I suggest we go back now and re-equip and re-group.'

Paul's eyes were distant and shining, like he was commanding some kind of phantom army and could already see his troops advancing.

'Operation Sheep poop, more like!' William commented, scraping his sandal on the ground. This brought smiles from the others and sniggers from his brother. 'What's wrong with him, anyway?' William prodded at Patrick who was still laying flat down. Patrick wriggled crabwise away from

133

the poking toe, and continued to lie, hands muffing his ears, face down in the dust and dirt. 'He's crazy, I'm telling you.' William shook his head. 'He ought to be put away!'

To underline the point, he screwed a finger into the side of his head and Trevor began capering round, eyes crossed, tongue lolling out of the side of his mouth. William joined in. They were both high, relieved from the terror they too had felt, putting their fear onto Patrick.

'That's what our dad says,' William leaned over him, yelling into his ear. 'Our dad don't like us playing with him. Says he's too big to play with us little kids. Says he's a danger and—'

'Ought to be in the loony bin!' Trevor joined in on the other side of the prone figure. 'Ought to be put away!'

Under this double assault, Patrick jumped up and fled, leaping and crashing through the barley like some ungainly hare.

'Now look what you've done!' Paul screamed at them. 'You're out of the gang. You know that? As of now!'

'As of, so what?' William's upper lip curled in contempt. 'We don't want to be in your stinky gang, anyway! Operation Crash Site.' He threw his head back, parodying Paul's pronouncement. 'Operation Crap Site, that's what I'd call it! You're mad, Paul Jordan! As mad as your barmy brother!'

'Cracked the pair of you!' Trevor shouted over his shoulder as they ran away. 'Crazy! Crazy! Bats in the belfry!'

They charged off down the field, whooping and shrieking like Red Indians. Nigel and Ian turned to follow.

'Where are you two going?'

'It's getting hot,' Ian turned back. Drops beaded his forehead and upper lip. He wiped his face with his shirt sleeve. 'And it'll be dinner soon. We better be going back.'

134

'What about this after?'

'Dunno.' He glanced at Nigel who looked away. 'Maybe. Dunno if I'll be playing out . . .'

'What about you?' Paul was talking to Nigel now.

'Might.' Nigel shrugged. 'I'll call round.'

'What time?'

'Dunno. It depends.'

'On what?'

'What we're going to do.' Nigel pushed at the glasses slipping down his nose. 'I don't see the point of coming up here again, not if we can't get in.'

'Me, neither,' Ian nodded his agreement. 'We'll more than likely get caught and my dad says—'

'I was thinking of going at night,' Paul said, desperate not to lose them.

'Maybe.' They both shrugged.

'My mum might not let me. Not after the last time . . .'

'Nor mine, I'll have to see.' Nigel gave the club sign, circling thumb and forefinger. 'See you later.'

'Alligator.'

'No! Wait!' Paul could not believe his troops were deserting. He went to run after them, but I pulled him back.

'Leave them for now. We've got to get Patrick.'

We ploughed through the waist-high barley, following the ragged track Patrick had made in his flight from the taunting twins. Near to the hedge the bearded fronds stood tall, but in towards the centre of the field large sweeps of grain had been flattened in swirling circles.

'We better find him quick,' Paul stared round, eyes widening at the damage to the crop. 'If Harley gets to him first, he'll shoot him. Us, too, for that matter.'

'Hang about,' I turned, looking at the flattened stalks. 'Patrick couldn't have done this. The area is far too big.'

135

'You're right! These are crop circles! I've read about this, but never seen it.' He seemed more excited about this than finding Patrick. 'Look at the way they lead off from each other, spiralling from one to another. Look at the way all the stems lie the same way.'

I looked about, then down to the ground. They could have been caused by storm damage, but now he pointed it out, they did look rather machined and precise. Patrick was in the middle of the last one, arms wrapped round himself, whirling and spinning in his own personal circle dance. As we got closer, he suddenly collapsed, folding to the floor, body rigid, and lay there, staring straight up into the air. Paul and I looked at each other. We both thought the same: he was having a fit or something and we would never be able to get him back from here.

We had to get right up to see that nothing like that was wrong with him. He hadn't passed out. He was just lying down. There was only one thing to do. I joined him in the middle of the circle and stared up into the deep clear blue.

It was not uncomfortable. The stalks of barley lay bent over, not broken like stubble, more woven and flat like a raffia mat.

'Hi, Patrick,' I started conversationally. 'What are you doing?'

'Listen,' he said, dismissing my question with a shake of his head, holding up his hand for silence.

'To what exactly?'

'To those.' He pointed at small flies hovering like tiny helicopters. 'Can't you hear it?'

'Hear what? All I can hear is buzzing.'

'It's not buzzing.' He shook his head from side to side. 'That's what they want you to think. Look how they move.'

'What about it?'

'There and there and there and back? 45 degrees each time, adds up to 360 degrees. A complete circle.'

'So?'

'They are not flies at all. They are miniature cameras equipped with transmitters. That's what the buzzing sound is.'

I recognized the insects as hover-flies, but I had never really looked at them before. Now I focused on them completely: the bulbous eyes, huge in relation to size; the turning choreographed dance; the blurring wings beating impossibly fast. I understood. I could see how Patrick could think it; but such a thing was impossible.

'Don't be silly, Patrick,' I said gently. 'Cameras are great big things, with long cables which have to be plugged in. You could never make one as small as that.'

'We couldn't. But they are not going to be the same as us. I think they're parked up somewhere and have sent those little cameras out to spy on us.'

'Where do you think they are?' I asked.

'Over there,' he indicated with a wave of his hand. 'Past the danger signs, beyond the trees, where the digging is. Men are trying to get at their craft. My guess is that they probably won't even find it.'

'Why not?'

'Because they won't be in our dimension,' he said patiently, as if explaining to a child. 'They must be able to switch between dimensions to get here at all. They must have a different way of travelling. It would take rockets like ours millions and millions of years to make such a journey. They would decay to dust long before they reached their destination.'

'If they can change dimensions, how come they are stuck here?'

'I don't know. Maybe they need to make repairs. Maybe they are stopping for a bit because they like it. Maybe they're collecting.' He paused. 'I think they've been here before.'

'What makes you think that?'

'They suck your brains out. Paul told me,' he said in the same matter-of-fact way.

I did not respond, just lay next to him trying to follow the direction of the conversation. Talking to Patrick was like that. His mind went its own way, but he wasn't so hard to understand, if you were prepared to follow his lead.

'That's how I know they were here before.'

'How? I don't quite see.'

'Last time, they took part of mine,' he explained in his careful way. 'The part that makes me the same as other people. They come through the window in my room. That's why I nailed it up. I use the crawl space to get away, but that does not always work.' He stared up at the sky. 'I've been thinking about it and I've decided that's what has happened and now I want it back. Either that, or,' he closed his eyes and his voice sounded far away and tired, 'I don't want to stay here any more. Sometimes they take people away, Paul told me. I want them to take me. I want to go with them.'

'Pat, Jo,' Paul was running over to us. 'Get up both of you. We've got to go.'

'No,' Patrick replied, still with closed eyes. 'They made these circles in the corn. I'm waiting for them to come and get me . . .'

'Not now, Pat. You can't,' Paul's voice was edging towards panic. 'We've got to get out of here. Harley's spotted us!'

I sat up. I could hear a man shouting, dogs barking. 'They won't come now, Patrick,' I shook his arm, not sure

138

*how he would react to me touching him, but we had to get him out of there. 'We might as well go.'*

Patrick rose onto his elbows, propping himself up. He looked straight at me with eyes the colour of the sky. 'When will be the right time?'

'Later,' I was on my feet. 'We'll come back later.'

'You promise?'

'Yes. Soon. I promise.' The barking was getting nearer. I bent down, close to the ground, pulling Patrick after me. 'But we have to get out of here now.'

It was nearly midday by the time we got back. No dogs barked here, no birds sang. There was no one around as we entered our cul-de-sac. It was possible to believe that everyone had been abducted; that we were returning, lone survivors to a deserted planet. The sky was white. The middle distance shimmered like a desert. As we walked along, two dark figures began to emerge in front of us, wobbly and shimmering as from a mirage. As they drew nearer, their bodies grew more solid. Two men. Both dressed in black despite the heat. Each wore a dark suit and sunglasses under a broad brimmed hat.

Paul stopped, motioning for us to fall back behind him.

'What's the matter?' I asked. 'What's up?'

'Shh! Shut up!'

The two men were nearly at our house. Before I could say another thing, Paul pulled us into next door's privet hedge. We crouched down, sheltering under the dark green leathery leaves, breathing in the sharp, rank smell. The men were going up the path to our house. I peered through the lattice work of twigs. They were in the porch. Ringing the bell.

Paul put a finger to his lips for absolute silence and crept forward, straining to pick up what was being said.

'Sorry to disturb you, Ma'am. If we could take up just a few moments of your time.'

The voice sounded strange, foreign. I'd never heard anyone speak like that, apart from in films and on the television. The man was American. They spoke one after another. Turn and turn about. One picked up where the other left off.

'We've come to bring you a message.'

'A warning to you and your family.'

'Tell me, Ma'am, how many people live in this house with you?'

The men stopped speaking then and appeared to be listening. I could hear my mother's voice but not what she was saying.

'Bear with us a moment, we have something important—' There was the click of a case opening.

'Please, Ma'am, we urge you to . . .' The rest of the conversation was lost to us as they moved further inside the porch.

'Thank you for your time.' They were stepping back now, preparing to leave.

'Please remember what we have said.'

'Bear it in mind.'

'We will be back.'

The door closed. The men came down the drive and turned right. They walked off along the road without a backward glance.

Paul still would not let us show ourselves. We remained huddled under the privet.

'Why can't we go? We'll be late for dinner—' I began to get up. Paul yanked me back.

'Men In Black,' he muttered.

'What?'

'Sinister visitors who turn up after UFO sightings and call on possible witnesses. Stay where you are. It's not safe yet.'

A car engine started further up the street and a big dark car swished past. The driver and his passenger stared straight ahead, still with their hats on, their faces blank, impassive, dark glasses fixed on the road.

'What are they doing here?' I asked.

'It went over this way,' Paul hissed. 'The flying saucer. We saw it. Me and Patrick. Now they've come after us. They work for the government . . .'

Patrick scrunched even further down at that, hands over his ears again, legs folded like penknives. We all stayed low, keeping still and hidden, until the car's engine had faded into the distance. Paul waited until he was completely certain that they had gone before popping his head round the hedge.

'All clear,' he breathed. 'That was a near thing.' He whistled his relief, crawling back into the dark, dusty safety of the privet. 'Now we have to see what's out there at the crash site. It's absolute top priority. This is what we'll do . . .'

Paul talked on about crashed craft, UFOs, Men in Black, outlining his plan to get to the bottom of it all. Paul had to reassure Patrick several times that the car had gone completely, but now he was sitting up, arms hugging his knees, listening intently, nodding at everything his brother said. I heard a noise above me and looked up to see the twins grinning down from their upstairs window. They were hanging out of it, listening too, trying to contain spluttering giggles. I suddenly realized how ridiculous we must look. Cowering in hedges, hiding from what?

141

'Oi, Jordan, you're trespassing,' one of them shouted. Paul and Patrick jumped a mile and they both hooted with laughter. 'What you hiding from? Little green men?' This witticism sent them off into fresh paroxysms.

'Maybe they've come up from the crash site specially. "We've come for Paul Jordan, 39 Woodside Close. All right, Missis, we'll wait." ' Trevor put on a squeaky staccato and they both broke up, whinnying and snorting.

'Crapsite, crapsite,' they began to chant, then their tone changed. 'We went and there was nothing there,' William leaned out further, jeering at Paul.

'Yeah. We did our dare. Now it's your turn,' his twin joined in. They both stared down at us, heads tilted back, their eyes dark slits, their mouths split in identical goofy grins.

'You've got to do your promise. Don't think that we've forgotten, because we haven't. We want to see it.' He mimed a gun, aiming at us with forefinger and thumb.

'And the you-know-whats,' Trevor reminded his brother.

'Yeah, and them, too. Without them it don't count.'

'Yeah, we dare you,' Trevor shouted. 'Now you better hop it. Next door don't want loonies in their garden, so get out.'

# Chapter 18

SUMMER.DOC completely absorbed Josh. He forgot about the game, Katherine and everything else. The only thing he kept in mind was the time. He did not have all that long. He periodically checked the bottom corner of the screen. Mum could return at any minute and then he would not be able to get back in again. As he read through, he noted down details and then printed the pages to refer to later. When the story ended, he shut the computer down, went into the lounge and began looking through his UFO magazines. He picked up his pad again and began to make notes.

*UFO: ASSOCIATED PHENOMENON*
*Crashed Saucer Overview: UK Retrievals*
*US – most heavily documented events.*
*UK – Cumbria, North Yorks. Moors, Rendlesham Forest.*
*First reports late 50s/early 60s.*
*So it's possible.*
*Animal Mutilation*
*Strange injuries suffered by horses, cattle and sheep. Aliens collecting earth life forms? Experimentation?*
*Reported worldwide. US esp. Montana and Texas.*
*UK – Northern Ireland & North Wales.*

*\* Strange lights and black helicopters seen in the skies before and during mutilations.*

<u>*Crop Circles*</u> *– areas of corn, barley, grass, etc. flattened in a circular pattern.*

*Not widely reported until 1980s. But there are older cases (Australia – 1966) & Hertfordshire Mowing Devil, 1678!!*

*\* Associated phenomenon: lights in sky, singed or burnt trees nearby.*

*\*\* Crop not just flattened. Stalks often reported to be bent, not broken and to have a woven or even plaited appearance.*

<u>*Mystery Helicopter*</u> *– Helicopters routinely reported at or around events or sightings. Sometimes 'black' (unmarked). Sometimes belonging to the military.*

<u>*Men in Black*</u> *– Mystery visitors, usually travel in twos. Dressed in black suits, hats, dark glasses, arrive in black car. Visit potential witnesses of an event/encounter, abductees, etc. Opinion divided as to whether MIB are govt. employees, or some kind of alien spy network.*

*\* MIB visits especially associated with 50s.*

<u>*Alien Abduction*</u> *– Incidents where abductees (or experiencers) report being transported from their bedrooms (or cars) and taken (usually at night) aboard alien space craft, where weird things are done to them – experiments, etc. Many abductees only realize what has happened when they discover a gap in their lives – 'missing time'.*

*\* Some abductees, particularly repeaters (those taken multiple times) shut themselves into small confined spaces to try and escape –* e.g. crawl way???

While he was looking through his notes again, the doorbell rang. It was Katherine. He had been so absorbed in his research that he had forgotten all about her.

'Sorry I'm late,' she said as she came in. 'I have something awful to confess.'

'Oh, what's that?'

She bit her lip. 'Promise you won't be angry?'

'Depends what it is,' Josh said gruffly, but really he was too glad she was here to be cross at all.

'I've been playing the game.'

'Is that all?'

'Why?' She looked at him curiously. 'What were you expecting?'

'Oh, nothing.' Josh couldn't very well admit to his fears about the skater guy. He had absolutely no call on Katherine. Who she saw and how she spent her time were nothing to do with him. What right had he to be jealous?

'What have you been doing?' Katherine asked.

'Mum wrote some more of her story. I've been reading that.'

'Really? May I see?'

'Sure. I printed it out.' He passed the pages over to her. 'Here, help yourself. Do you want a cup of tea?'

'Yeah, love one,' Katherine said without looking up. She was already reading through the latest instalment of SUMMER.DOC.

When he came back she was sitting cross-legged on the floor, leafing through the UFO magazines, absorbing them one after another.

'So?' He sat on the floor opposite. 'What do you think?'

'Hang on a minute. Let's have a look at those.' She held out a hand for Joshua's notes.

'I know what you're going to say,' Josh said defensively, remembering her scepticism the previous day.

145

'Do you now?' Katherine smiled over her tea.

'Yes. You're going to say that there could easily be rational explanations for all these phenomena.' He marked them off on his fingers. 'The mutilated sheep might not necessarily have been experimented on by aliens. It could have been attacked by a dog. The crop circles could be storm damage. The helicopter is just that, a helicopter.'

'You forgot the Men in Black.'

'Oh. Yes. They were probably Jehovah's Witnesses. Anyway,' Josh went on, 'I know all that, so please don't patronize me.'

'I wasn't going to.'

'I know you think it's all weird—'

'I didn't say that,' she smiled at him. 'Anyway, that's not what I think is weird.'

'What is, then?'

'You've got so hung up on UFOs and aliens you can't see it, can you?'

'See what?'

'The weirdest thing is the game. And this.' She collected up the pages of the copy of SUMMER.DOC and held them up to him. 'The similarity. I thought it was strange yesterday, but now,' she shivered slightly, 'it's totally uncanny.'

'Uncanny?' Josh looked up at her. 'In what way?'

'They are about the same thing, Joshua,' she paused to let her words sink in. 'It's not just the house. The setting. The story and the game . . . they relate to the same incident. They are about the same events.'

'How can you be sure?'

'I can't be absolutely, but, even apart from the tiles, there's other stuff as well.'

'Such as?'

'Things in the game. Clues, if you like. Things I didn't understand. Like labyrinths made of plaited straw,' she numbered them on her fingers. 'Maggots crawling over everything. Menacing black figures that fill the screen. Tiny flying bugs that transmit pictures and turn into helicopters.'

Josh got up from the floor and went towards the dining room. 'I think you'd better show me.'

Josh started the game but, no sooner had he done so, the screen went black.

'What's wrong?' Kath moved her chair nearer, looking over his shoulder.

'It's a lockup.' Josh clicked the mouse frantically and pounded the keys. The screen remained frozen. Nothing happened. 'This machine's rubbish. It's done this before. Mum's got too many programs on it.'

'What do we do now?'

'Start it up again.'

'Go on, then.'

Josh did so, several times, but each time the same thing happened. 'We could go back to your house.'

Katherine shook her head. 'My sister's got her mates round, they'll be crawling all over us: "I want to play! I want to play!" ' She put on a lisping little-girl voice.

'We could always shut the door.'

'You saw them the other day. They'd have it off the hinges.' She sat back on her chair, arms folded, thinking, then she said, 'This story your mum's writing is about her, when she was a kid, right?'

Josh nodded.

'Well, we could ask her.'

'But she's not here. And even if she was, we couldn't.'

'Why not?'

Josh ran his hands through his hair. 'She wouldn't like it. She'd go ape if she even *thought* we'd been reading her stuff. She sees it as prying. She's told me not to and I don't want to upset her. She's got a lot on her mind just now.'

It was difficult to explain. Joanna regarded her writing as an extremely private activity and, at the moment especially, she seemed to be more than usually troubled, preoccupied.

'OK. There is only one other thing we can do,' Katherine stood up.

'What's that?'

'Go down the library. Check how much of it is true. I don't think that we're going to find "Alien Invasion: Special Edition" but they've got old maps there and newspapers on microfilm. We might be able to find out something. Come on. It's worth a try.'

The librarian slotted in the microfilm for 1959 and left them to it.

'Ever used one of these things?' Katherine asked as she whizzed the film along.

Josh shook his head.

'They're good. Hang on.' She adjusted the control and the picture slowed down. 'June, July, August. 7, 14, 21 and 28.'

Josh looked at the screen. 'Are you sure that's the front page?'

'Yes. Look at the top.'

'It's covered in adverts.'

'That's the way papers were back then. Now it should go sports, sports, women's page, news.' The pages scrolled under her hand.

'What exactly are we looking for?'

'Any kind of support to what your mum says happened and I don't mean "UFOs on Yarndale Common", especially since most of the land it's supposed to have crashed on had probably gone. See? Look at that!'

'What?' Josh frowned, puzzled. All he could see was an article about building a motorway.

'And that!' She pointed at an idealized sketch of a proposed town centre development. 'Ripping up the countryside for roads, tearing down the town. 50s, 60s, that was when the damage was done. Civic vandalism. Destroying all the old buildings to put up awful shops and the concrete rubbish bin we're in now.' She gestured round at the low-ceilinged open-planned expanse of the Central Library.

'That one of the things you're into, the environment?' Josh asked, wanting to know more about her, but not wanting to get side-tracked.

'Uhuh. One of them.' Katherine's eyes remained fixed on the screen. 'Hey, look what's on at the cinema.'

Josh leaned closer to read the item.

### Palace Cinema: Forthcoming Attractions

On the last four days of this week, the Palace Cinema follows its showing of 'The Spider' and 'The Brain Eaters' with more science fiction horror in the form of 'The Blob' and 'I Married a

Monster from Outer Space'. Both films take place in small American townships and continue the theme of alien beings terrorizing young and old alike.

Katherine looked up. 'Quite a coincidence, eh?'

Josh nodded.

'What's that?' Josh directed her gaze. 'Further down the page.'

'Where? Oh, yeah. "Storm caused a fire and damage to crops",' she read out. 'We've got the right edition. This must be the one Ian brought to the meeting. This is the article your mum read out to the gang in the shed. We'll have that. Well spotted Boy Wonder. Stick 30p in there and I'll print it out.'

'So there was a storm,' Josh said as he took the copy. 'And it says here that a sub-station was hit, so there was a blackout.' His mother's story was being borne out. 'What shall we do now?'

'You go and look at the maps. I'll stay here, see what more I can find. There might be something about sheep-worrying.'

'What about?'

'Excuse me?'

Josh looked down at her, his face expressionless. 'The sheep. What were they worrying about?'

'Oh! Joke!' She laughed. 'Ha, ha! Well, if I was them, I'd be a lot more worried about marauding dogs than alien experimentation.'

'You were right.' Josh spread out the maps he'd photo-copied. 'This is then, 1959. Notice all the green fields? Hardly a building in sight. And now . . .' He put a second map on top of the first to show how the land had been neatly parcelled up and divided. 'That whole area has all been swallowed in new development. Harley's Farm is now "The Harleys", a new executive housing estate. Painter's Wood is Painter's Business Park, and Yarndale Common disappeared under the motorway. I reckon that could be significant,' he said looking down at the map. 'See? It's up in this corner.' He pointed to the upper right portion of the map. 'Kathy, Kath? Are you listening?' She nodded. 'Did you find anything?'

'I found out about the helicopter. Some kind of bigwig on a visit.'

'Oh, right.' He grinned. 'Did you find what the sheep were worrying about?'

She nodded absently. 'Pack of dogs roaming the area.' Her voice sounded odd, slow and mechanical. 'That's probably why Harley carried a gun. I found this, too.' Katherine turned a sheet over. A facsimile page from the newspaper. 'And this,' she turned another sheet. 'And this.'

She laid the copies out in front of him. They were all dated from the first weeks of September, 1959. The headlines changed from: 'LOCAL CHILD MISSING' to: 'HOPE FADES'.

Josh's smile died as his eyes scanned the stories. He read them twice and then again. In the sparse matter-of-fact prose of local journalism, they told of how a child had gone out to play one hot August day, and had never been seen again. The photo was the same each time. Sometimes bigger, sometimes smaller, depending on the prominence of the story on the page. A school snap, of the kind they took back in those days. Josh had seen ones of his mother. Just head and shoulders, staring straight at the camera. The shirt collar too big for the neck, one corner slightly turned up, pulled in by a narrow striped tie in a tight, twisted knot. The hair neatly parted, fixed with a hint of Brylcreem, falling onto a wide, high forehead. The whole angle of the head was tilted back. The light clear eyes were half closed, as though the subject was jeering at the camera. The face was small, triangular, split by a wide grin showing prominent white teeth, separated by gaps, too big for the mouth. The ears stuck out, too, at almost forty-five-degree angles. They were smaller than Josh had imagined from his mother's description. Little cup shapes attached to the side of the head.

The photograph was of nine-year-old William Henry James, of 35, Woodside Close. Josh sat back in his chair feeling slightly sick. He had not expected this. Up until now, finding out about what had happened had been like the game, solving a mystery, a series of puzzles. But this was not some elaborate kind of brainteaser, this was real.

Josh had to look again, just to make absolutely certain. When he first saw the name, he thought that there must be a mistake, that they had got the wrong one.

# Chapter 19

*Gone to the library – be back later.*

Joanna read the note left for her on the hall table. Probably just as well. She had to find Patrick's death certificate, the solicitor was insistent, he could not proceed further without it. This meant a thorough search of her father's desk, his room, the whole house probably, and she would be better doing that by herself.

She pulled out the desk drawers one after another, rifling the contents: odds and ends, old pens, unused stationery, sheaves of correspondence related to his business. Nothing of interest. The brass handle on the bottom right hand side would not give. The drawer was locked. Joanna frowned, checking through every key she had, none of them fitted. The paperknife was not strong enough to force it. She went to the kitchen to fetch a screwdriver.

She forced the metal point into the gap between the edge of the drawer and the body of the desk and levered. The lock popped and the drawer jerked open with a splintering of pale oak. She was damaging the fabric of the desk but she didn't care. The drawer was full of correspondence, much of it unopened, thrown in anyhow. Most of the envelopes appeared to be official, brown with cellophane windows, dating back donkey's years by the look of the stamps.

Joanna read the sender's address on the back and shut her eyes, like she used to as a kid, in the faint hope that whatever troubled her would be gone when she opened them up again. Then it worked, sometimes. It never worked now. She held on to the side of the desk willing herself not to pass out. Her legs were shaking and she felt sick, breathless, as if she had swallowed something poisonously cold. She hung on tight waiting for the world to right itself. Perhaps she ought to phone Paul? But he would be at work. Perhaps she should . . .

Except it was too late for that, anyway. Too late to do anything.

Too late now, the words chimed in her head as she stared down at the envelopes. She scooped them all out, cleared a space on the dining room table. Too late by a lifetime, she thought, as she placed them in order.

Joanna stood for another second, undecided, and then picked up a paper knife. Hands trembling, she slit open the first envelope. She did not need to read past the first paragraph to know what information the writer had to offer about the fate of her brother. She put the letter down and got up, unable to sit any longer, but as soon as she stood, she had the sensation of falling. She stared at her whitened knuckles on the back of the chair, willing herself not to faint. Who had known about this? Dad, certainly. What about her mother? She would not have looked in here when he was alive. She never questioned him about anything. But what about afterwards? Had she looked in this drawer and then slammed it shut? Or had she left it alone, along with the rest of his stuff? Joanna sighed and closed her eyes. She couldn't ask her now, that was for sure.

She made herself sit down again and read the letters carefully one after another. When she had finished, she put all the letters back in their envelopes and the envelopes back in order. The implications were enormous. So huge, they could not be seen entirely, only glimpsed a bit at a time. She would have to call Paul. He was involved as much as she was, as much as Patrick.

She went to the phone, but on the dialling tone she quietly replaced the receiver. She would have to talk to him soon, but not yet. Before doing that, she would have to travel back, find the right path among the crooked tracks of memory, and face the truth.

## CONTACT

*Inside the house the heat was stifling. I went up to my room and lay on the bed, dressed just in my underwear. Patrick found the only cool place, down in the hall, and lay staring at the floor. Mum warned him of the consequences if Dad found him like that, but he did not react. Paul was in a mood, still smarting from the twins' taunting. He had gone off by himself and was not there to help, so she had to leave Patrick where he was. He was too big for her to move by herself.*

*Dad came back at one o'clock, as he always did, for his lunch. He was slightly late, which always made him angry, and the heat had made his temper worse. To get to the dining room, he had to step over Patrick. He yelled at him* to get up. Again, Patrick took no notice but this time he was hauled to his feet and dragged into Dad's study to be given a good hiding. Mum and I stood outside, powerless.

'I warned him,' she was muttering it like a litany, more to herself than anyone else. 'I did warn him. I knew he'd come home out of sorts. The heat doesn't suit him and he thinks Patrick does it on purpose to provoke him.'

She did not try to intervene to stop what was going on; she spoke to drown out the swish and thunk as the swagger stick swung and connected. Patrick made no sound, but then he never did.

Dad came out, dragging Patrick by the collar. He was shaking him backwards and forwards, shouting, ordering him to his room, spittle flying, when the doorbell rang. Dad drove Patrick to the stairs and then went back down the hall, halting by the mirror to check his appearance, smooth his hair down, waiting for Mum to step forward. It was her job to answer the door.

It was those men again. The two we saw earlier. They were Mormons, Jehovah's Witnesses, something like that, hands full of tracts. From where I was standing, I could see that.

'Is your husband home, Ma'am?'

Before the words were fully spoken, Patrick let out a piercing scream and ran forward, babbling and shouting. Dad grabbed hold of him and dragged him up the stairs. Mum was left on the doorstep saying something like, 'Perhaps you could call back tomorrow?' It would have been funny if it had not been tragic.

Dad did not use the stick. This time he locked Patrick in. Patrick hated being confined, so Dad had put a bolt outside the attic door: 'The only way to teach him a lesson.' We had been told to ignore Patrick raging up there, smashing things, kicking the wall. In the house, Dad ruled. Inter-ference would have been open defiance, a serious offence with a punishment to match. Neither Paul nor I were prepared to invite that. We waited for Dad to go back to work and then we sneaked upstairs with orange squash and fish paste sandwiches pinched from lunch. The bolt was still on the door but the attic was empty.

Paul checked the crawl space. Patrick liked it in there; he felt safe and he could come out when he wanted to. He sometimes hid there when he was badly frightened. He was not there this time, though. The roof space was empty, too. He must have got down through one of the trap doors in the ceilings below. He'd done it before. He was as thin and wriggly as an eel. Paul came back out, pale and frowning.

'What's up? What's the matter?'

'It's the haversack. The one for tonight, for the expedition. I put it in there for safe keeping. He's taken it.'

'So?' Patrick liked cases, haversacks, things like that. 'He'll bring it back.'

'It's not that,' Paul bit his lip. 'It's what I put in it.'

'Like what?'

'Things I'd rather Patrick didn't get his hands on.'

'Such as?'

'A torch,' Paul shrugged, 'wire cutters, matches and . . .' He paused, his face whiter still, then he went on, 'and the gun.'

'Not Dad's one?'

He nodded.

'Oh, no! What ever possessed you?'

'I put it in to show them.' His face went dark and stubborn. 'To show the twins I wasn't scared. That I could do the dare.'

'What about bullets?' I asked, already knowing the

157

*answer. That had been part of it. Paul did not say anything.
He just sat back on his heels, his head sunk down between
his knees.*

   *'We'd better find him,' I shook his shoulder. 'Come on,
Paul!' I shook him harder. 'We have to find him, quick.'*

*It was a hot afternoon. Outside the air was still, nothing
moved. Perhaps it was my anxiety inside, or a trick of
the light, but the landscape seemed drier, more desiccated,
bleached and white, drained of colour. The leaves hung
limp, crisping at the edges as we went down the garden
towards the brook. It was the route Paul had planned;
Patrick was likely to stick to that. We crept along the bottom
of the gardens. Paul motioned caution when we got to the
twins' house. There was no sign of them, just toys strewn
about, ray guns and stuff like that, as if they'd been out
playing some game and had then abandoned it. We went
on to the bridge and then under the road, following the
stream again.*

   *We stopped and listened. We were on Harley's land now,
and had to be on the alert, but there was no one about and
it was too hot even for dogs to be out. We crossed the stream
via the stepping stones. Paul cast round for footprints, but
it was a place where cattle came down to drink and the
churned mud had all but dried out. There were a couple of
squashed bits which could have been shoe prints, but
nothing conclusive.*

   *We carried on up the slope until stopped by the barbed
wire fence. Paul traced it along until he came to a gap. He
smiled grimly, pointing to where a section had been cut out.
Patrick must have used the cutters from the haversack. That
proved we were on the right track. Paul went through first
and I was about to follow when I noticed some strands of*

material snagged on the wire. Green threads. I took one between finger and thumb. It felt like T-shirt cotton. I called to Paul but he shouted for me to come on. We were now the wrong side of the danger signs. It was all open, clear up the sloping fields to the crest of Painter's Wood. If anyone was going to see us, it would be here.

We kept low, running up the hill as fast as we could, not stopping until we got to the edge of the wood. We came to a halt at the entrance, and bent over, hands on thighs, to catch our breath. Gradually we straightened up, breathing normally, but still we stood there, each reluctant to enter. There was no wind, no breeze at all, but the tops of the trees were in constant motion, rustling, as though whispering one to another. There were big warning signs, 'DO NOT ENTER' nailed high up on some of the tree trunks. Paul passed beneath them and I followed him on into the wood.

The trees thinned, light showing through them. We crept to the very edge of the wood and then hung back. There was no sign of Patrick. We should have been looking at Yarndale Common, but in front of us all the trees had gone, reduced to splintered stumps, root systems turned up, fanning out from toppled stubs. It looked like a war zone. All the way around, in every direction, the earth was bare of vegetation, gouged and churned up. The ground rose up to a broken ridge and then disappeared completely. The landscape had been changed utterly, ripped through and torn apart as if by some great force, some terrible explosion.

'I told you something had happened, didn't I?' Paul whispered to me. 'Now do you believe?' He dropped down to his knees then onto his belly. We edged and crawled, worming our way like commandos, inching towards the rim and whatever lay beyond it.

*The crater's edge crumbled away from us. We lay, staring down into a cauldron carved out of the hillside. Fields, hedges, trees had all disappeared, replaced by a great pit of bare earth. I had never seen anything like it. The sides rose sheer and at the bottom great machines rested on wheels as big as houses. Cranes stood poised, their jibs swinging like compass needles. Massive concrete mixers stood like fat-bellied dinosaurs. There were lights, twice, three times as tall as street lights. Prefabricated buildings were scattered about, some oblong, like caravans, others long and wide, like aircraft hangars. By my side, Paul was squinting down into the site, using his hands like binoculars.*

*'It all fits,' he whispered. 'Isolate the craft at the crash site. It's probably in there,' he pointed to the hangar-like place, 'or down one of those shafts,' he indicated a series of black squares rimmed with steel girders. 'They can study it before moving it out using the cranes and those big machines.'*

*I looked again. We did not seem to be seeing the same thing. In the time it took for the eye to blink, I understood. We were not watching a film, or looking at frames in a comic book. This was no UFO crash site. There was no pulsing pit on the edge of town, no incubating pods, no invading hordes waiting to take over the world. Those weren't holding shafts, they were just holes driven deep to provide the foundations for the bridge that would one day span that particular section of the motorway. Childhood's spell fell away from me; the one that says everything is what you want it to be, anything else is an adult conspiracy. Paul talked on. I stayed dumb at his side, no longer listening.*

*I scanned the area below, quartering it, searching for movement. 'Where is Patrick?' I shouted. 'I don't see* him . . . Wait.' I grabbed Paul's arm. 'We've been looking in the wrong place.'

I directed my gaze diagonally across the site to the face of the horseshoe-shaped cliff opposite, which marked the centre point of the earth-shifting activity eating its way through what was left of Yarndale Common. It was in deep shadow, and at least fifty metres to our right, but I caught a movement there and picked up a figure, climbing up the side of the precipice. Long arms, long legs, spider thin. It had to be Patrick. He must have got down to the bottom somehow, and now he was climbing back out. Paul cupped his hands round his mouth to shout, but I restrained him. Any distraction and Patrick might fall. Hardly breathing, we watched his progress. Hand over hand, effortlessly moving from one hold to another, he swarmed up the slope in front of him. Patrick was a good climber because he did not know physical fear.

'He's going to be fine,' I said. 'He's going to be OK.'

We got up to go and meet him. That's when I noticed another figure. It was squatting on its heels, perched at the top of the crater looking down into the pit. It looked like an imp. Then it stood and I saw that it was not an imp at all. It was one of the twins dressed in a zip-up suit. The kind they wore to play little green men from outer space. It had to be one of them. I could see the white ping pong ball antennae bobbing about as the figure crept with exaggerated stealth along the edge of the crater to a point near where Patrick was set to appear.

The effect was comic. I was almost laughing. I felt no foreboding. No warning bells went off in my head. If they had, perhaps I could have prevented what happened. All I remember thinking was that it had to be William, because Trevor was afraid of heights. As I watched, the little figure

161

reached down, took a stone or a clod of earth, and threw it at Patrick, hitting him on the head. Patrick looked up, he was nearly at the top. The little figure jumped in the air, star-shaped against the white glare. Patrick started back; I thought he was going to fall, but he held on with one hand. With the other, he grabbed for something in his waistband with the fluid grace of a gun slinger. There was a sharp crack, like something brittle snapping in the still air. Then another and another. I didn't know what it was. I'd never heard a gun shot.

The little figure was falling, arms flailing, tumbling from the top of the cliff. It fell past Patrick, but he did not look to see what it was or where it went. He just carried on climbing until he got to the top, then he heaved himself up over the edge and began walking away, dwindling to nothing, disappearing to a little black dot against the fierce light of the sun. We peered over into the chasm, searching for the other, smaller figure down among the tangle of uprooted trees and shrubs, the scree of huge boulders which littered the sloping cliff face. We could see nothing.

Paul grabbed at me, pointing to sudden activity. All had been deserted before, but now vehicles were driving about, men in helmets springing out.

'They must have heard the shots,' Paul said, 'been deployed to investigate.'

But he was wrong. They were intent on other business. They looked carefully along the cliff, scrutinising the face from one end to the other. At first, I thought Paul was right, that they had seen what happened and were looking for a body, looking for the twin, but then one of the men waved a red flag, another signalled back, and then another, and another, all across the site. He held his thumb up and the trucks headed back to the shelter of the central area. A siren sounded, its long drawn-out warning howling through the confined space. A series of tiny white dots of white smoke puffed from the base of the cliff where William had fallen.

I turned to Paul, opening my mouth to speak, but my words were swallowed up in a series of deafening explosions, so loud and so close together it was almost impossible to tell them apart.

The ground beneath us shook and convulsed. Across the chasm, the cliff face shivered and all along its length hundreds, thousands of tons of rock and earth fell with a deafening roar that seemed to snatch the air away. We threw ourselves back, lying down flat, arms over our heads, as an enormous cloud of grey dust ballooned outwards, turning day into night, reducing the sun to a feeble disc, threatening to engulf us.

We stood slowly, supporting each other, and stared across at a cliff that no longer existed. Paul's eyes met mine. They were all pupil, irises reduced to a thin grey rind. Moving as in a dream, we turned on shaking legs and went away from the place. We didn't go down and tell the men what had happened; we did not go home and tell our mother; we just kept on walking. Slowly at first, tottering on weak toddler legs, then faster and faster. It was as if our brains had shut down under protest, refusing to process what we had witnessed. Our thoughts were a spreading blankness. Our minds, unable to make sense of what we had seen, refused to weigh up consequences and work out proper courses of action. All we could think of was to get away.

'Later. We'll tell later,' Paul whispered, and we went, hand in hand, like Hansel and Gretel, into the woods, going deeper and deeper, until we found a quiet place, a hidden place. There, we curled up in the dry leaves, huddled together, holding onto each other. I don't know how long *we stayed like that. Hours went by in a blink of an eye. Time was erased. We came round to near-darkness and the sound of rain pattering down, bringing to an end that long, hot summer, putting an end to our childhood.*

# Chapter 20

Josh and Katherine got back from the library to find a brief note, '*At the solicitors*'. Josh crumpled it up, swearing under his breath. 'Not again! She's practically living there. I don't know why she doesn't move in.'

They went into the dining room. It was a mess, papers all over the place.

'Good thing *I* didn't leave it that way. One rule for us, one rule for them. That's just typical.'

'Perhaps she was looking for something,' Katherine suggested. 'There's a lot to sort out when someone dies.'

'I wanted to ask her about this,' Josh waved the newspaper article.

'Well, you can't because she's not here.'

'And I'm starving.'

'Get yourself something to eat, then. Even you can't be that helpless. You can get me something, too,' Katherine sat down at the computer. 'While I see if she's written any more.'

'Have you finished?' Josh asked in a quiet voice. They had been reading his mother's story together.

Katherine nodded. 'You'd better close the file.'

He executed the sequence quickly, but shutting it down was not shutting it out. The terrible scene his mother had witnessed lived on in his head. Images from what she had written came flashing back to him, as vivid as if he had been watching them on film.

Katherine sat next to him, subdued, still staring at the screen which was blank now, her arms folded, her half-eaten sandwich on the table by her elbow.

'This is true,' she said, almost to herself. 'Of course it's true.' Her hand touched the photocopies they had brought back from the library. 'We have the proof, don't we?' She passed her hand over her eyes. Josh thought there might have been tears there. 'When this started I never thought . . .'

'Neither did I,' Josh stared down miserably, running a fingernail along the worn grain at the edge of the table. 'If I had, I doubt I would have—'

'Yes, you would,' Katherine looked at him. 'You wanted to find out. And now you have.'

'But it's not what I thought . . .'

'Nothing ever is,' Katherine sighed. 'Maybe your mother was right, though, when she told you not to pry. I think we'd better tell her, come clean about what we've been doing.'

'No! I told you! She'd go crazy!'

'We've got to, Josh. Can't you see how serious this is? These things really happened. It's not like one of your games. To have witnessed something like that. All these years, having to live with it.'

'I know!' Josh was stung at how she could under-estimate him. 'It must have been terrible for her. And coming back now, going through it all again in her head, it must have been really bad. I know all that!'

'OK, I'm sorry. I didn't mean to get at you.' Katherine put her hand out to Joshua but he turned away from her, blinking and gripping the bridge of his nose, pinching away the tears collecting there.

'There's still the game,' Katherine said after a moment. 'If we get further on, it might tell us more. We might be able to work it out for ourselves, confirm once and for all that it's about the same event.'

'It's worth a try,' Josh managed a smile.

'It certainly is.' Katherine stood up.

'What if Mum comes back?'

'Then we can ask her.'

Josh shook his head. 'But I don't want to, not yet.'

'Come on, then. We'll play it round at my house.'

## Alansom games present:
## AlienState 3
## HomeWorld

The title of the game and the name checks came up and broke apart. The screen dissolved into the grid pattern windows of the first scene.

'Did you save it when you finished?'

Katherine nodded.

Josh brought up the Systems Menu and selected the LOAD option. 'We should be able to start playing from the last saved scene. Excellent.' He nodded his appreciation at how far Katherine had got on her own. 'The further on, the better. Now. Let's see where we are.'

A red direction arrow glowed in the darkness of a narrow tunnel. Josh moved the mouse, edging forward. An obstacle appeared, oblong and squashy, filling the space in front of them. Two options flashed up: JUNK and SAVE. Josh clicked on the second quickly. In this game a slow decision risked termination.

A menu scrolled up the side of the screen, an inventory of useful things: torch, map, matches, binoculars, wire cutters, weapon. The haversack. Josh's heart missed a beat.

'Go on along for a bit,' Katherine instructed.

Josh did as he was told and found a trap door set into the floor. 'We appear to be over, I don't know, looks like a mountain ski slope and a lake.'

'Go right, go right,' Katherine pointed. 'There's a ledge. Get on that. See that pipe thing? Use that to swing down.'

'And what about dangling over a mountain?'

'Zoom out.'

'Oh, right.' Josh smiled slightly, he'd been scrambling down an old-fashioned lavatory cistern and was hanging over a toilet basin. A gamemaker with a sense of humour.

'Go left. Over to the window.'

Josh did as he was directed and suddenly they were out. Liberated from the confines of the house, the graphics changed. It was like they were in savannah. All the colours were yellows and browns. The point of view swooped and flew, eating up the parched landscape, speeding down pathways, swerving round corners, until it came to a halt beside the lap and flow of water.

'The brook!'

Josh brought up the inventory and clicked on the

168

MAP icon. A black wiggly line snaked up and under a bridge, skirted farm land and then disappeared off the edge of the map. A red glowing spot showed their present position.

He used the directional arrows to proceed, ignoring all distractions, keeping the fast flowing water on his lefthand side. Twice he was tempted to go to the side. Once he reversed direction, but there was nothing of significance to be gained, it seemed, so he just followed the stream under the bridge and out again, only to see:

**you are on the wrong side of the river!**

'Stepping stones!' he and Katherine said together.

The similarity between the game and his mother's story was getting stronger with every click of the mouse. Mum's account paralleled the events in the game so closely that it acted like a Hints book. But how could that be? Josh was sweating, he could not get his head round the strangeness of it . . .

'Come on,' Katherine nudged him. 'We can't stop now!'

Dogs barked and snarled in stereo, they were coming from both sides, jaws snapping. Josh wrenched his mind back to the screen in front of him, jumping to take evasive action. He had to give the game his full concentration. They were nearing the heart of the mystery, and this game was ruthless. Any lapses, any mistakes and they would be right back at the beginning.

They were halfway across the second field when Josh heard sounds again. Not dogs this time. Someone following? He did a U-turn and caught the hint of movement. He zoomed in on that part of the screen. Nothing. He turned the binoculars back, sweeping the area in front of him. Long, thin strands of light vibrated before him. He took out the cutters from the inventory. Wire whipped and curled leaving a gap, a little door to crawl through.

Trees barred the way ahead. Warning signs flashed up. Josh clicked on IGNORE. The path through the wood opened up. As he took it the soundtrack's rustles and creaks were joined by strange whistles and shrieks. There were no visual clues – the screen remained dappled woodland browns and greens – but the sound effects pushed up the sinister sense of threat. The noises could mean nothing: just wind in the leaves, animals moving, birds calling. Or it could mean someone following. Up ahead a light began to glow yellow-white and the trees thinned out. A high pitched whinnying made Josh's finger jump on the mouse. Again it was hard to read the sound. It could be a horse in a nearby field, could be snorting laughter.

A question flashed up on the screen: **Forward? Y/N**

Josh clicked 'yes' and the viewpoint began to glide across a wasteland dotted with jagged stumps and up turned trees, rutted with criss-crossing tracks leading up to a broken ridge. Before Josh could attain this objective a prompt message filled the screen.

## HAZARDOUS AREA
## Proceed? Y/N

Josh pressed 'yes'. It was the obvious thing to do.

The ground in front now opened up on a scene that reminded Josh of pictures he'd seen in sci-fi films or UFO magazines of locations like Dreamland, or Area 51. It even had the hard light and shade effects of the harsh desert sun. The ground was littered with military recovery vehicles. At first they were looking from above, then the point of view changed, travelling forward and down until they were at ground level. The screen filled with a perimeter fence. A 'Danger' sign flashed up like an error warning:

## RESTRICTED AREA
## NO TRESPASSING
## USE OF DEADLY FORCE AUTHORIZED
## Proceed? Y/N

Josh pressed 'yes' and a forward movement started, tracking along the length of the fence until he stopped it. Then the viewpoint swung round to spy through the chainlink. Using the binoculars as image enhancers, Josh cased the area.

'How do we get in?' Katherine asked.

'How do you know that we are supposed to?'

'It seems the most obvious thing.'

'OK. Here goes.'

Josh used the cutters from his Inventory, half expecting some kind of warning siren to terminate play, but nothing happened. All remained quiet as he stole through the wire. He moved to the centre of the site. A hangar off to the right looked a likely location. He approached with caution, working his way round it.

'How about using the door?' Katherine suggested. 'Simple solutions work when all else fails, you said so yourself.'

She was right. The handle gave at first try, he didn't even need a key. The reason was clear as soon as he got inside, the whole building was empty. Josh went through and out the other side. All locations on the site were the same. No matter how promising it might appear to be externally, there was nothing in any of them. Each place was unresponsive, there was nothing to interact with. None of the machines and vehicles worked. It was as if the whole area was inert, sleeping in the harsh sunlight, deserted.

'Maybe I've missed something.' Josh could feel the frustration mounting in him. 'Maybe I'd better go back.'

'You can't. Look.' She zoomed the camera out. The site was crawling with patrolling figures. Some had dogs with them.

'Cammo dudes.'

'What?'

'Camouflaged security guys who guard crash sites. Not to be messed with.'

The only way was up. Josh entered an area darkened by shadow and began to climb the cliff. Searching for handholds, he clicked on one ledge, then another, until he was nearly at the top. The little figures marching around below didn't seem to notice him. Time had been rolling, the sun had moved on, it was now directly above. Just as Josh was about to emerge from out of the shadow, boulders began to fall, bouncing around him. After so little activity, Josh drew back sharply and directed his gaze upwards. The sun broke over the ridge in a blinding flash. Haloed by the bright white light, a shape was emerging: small, grey, elongated.

A red warning message pulsed in the middle of the screen:

**EBE: Extraterrestrial Biological Entity**

A missile hurtled straight out followed by another message:

**incoming! incoming!
defend yourself
HOSTILE! HOSTILE!**

Josh acted without thinking. He grabbed the weapon from the Inventory and aimed it. Red and orange streaked across the screen in a staccato burst of sustained fire. The little grey figure was falling, tumbling down the slope and past him. The camera angle yawed and slewed. The image shuddered, like a hand-held camcorder losing its picture. Then the screen went black.

'What's happened?'

'I don't know,' Josh stared at the darkened screen. 'We'll have to go back to where we last saved it.'

But he made no moves, his hands stayed poised on the keys, he was remembering his mother's description of the little tumbling figure. Real lives mixed with make-believe. Same story, different points of view. It was so weird it gave him a sick feeling inside, like he'd had in the library. Déjà vu mixed with vertigo.

'Are you all right?' Katherine was staring at him.

'I've got a headache, that's all.'

'Do you want to stop?'

'Do you?'

Katherine looked away. 'In a way, I do. This feels too like trespassing.' She nodded towards the screen. 'It scares me. But in another way, I want to go on. I want to know what happens.'

'Stepped in so far . . .'

'Say again?'

'Nothing,' Josh shook his head. 'It's a play we did at school. *Macbeth*. It means there comes a point in anything when it's easier to go on than go back.'

'Brains as well as beauty, eh?' She gave him the ghost of a smile, before turning back to the screen. 'We've certainly reached that. And we can't go back. If you've got a headache, why don't I take over for a while? You go and get us a couple of Cokes. There's some in the fridge.'

# Chapter 21

Josh came back to find Katherine deep in a twisting golden labyrinth. The shining walls were chevroned, exquisitely woven and plaited. The effect was dazzling. The camera glided slowly, dreamily. Bird song and insects buzzing on the soundtrack added to the deep, relaxed feeling that this was the right place to be.

'How did you get there?'

'Skill.' Katherine grinned. 'It's where I got to last night. It's similar, but not the same.'

Katherine began to follow the winding maze. Side chambers invited detours, but she refused to be distracted. She took them firmly right to the heart of it. Here something glittered. Josh sat forward, thinking it might be a crystal. They had not come across one before, but that did not mean anything; they usually turned up somewhere or other. It was not a crystal, or anything of that sort. It was a pair of glittering insect eyes.

'Fix and rotate.'

'What?'

Josh took over. 'Here, let me do it.'

The eyes grew, filling the screen. Suddenly the point of view changed. Instead of looking in, they were looking outward. The screen broke into hundreds of faceted images. Close-ups of human faces: eyes smiling, crying, mouths talking, laughing. Parts of people: legs walking, hands holding, arms embracing; babies being picked up, toddlers in pushchairs, children playing. Lives on show against a restless background of streets, parks, houses, gardens, schools, hospitals, beaches and shopping centres. Snatches of noise faded in and out. Sampled laughter, music, traffic and talking provided a meaningless soundtrack. Human life played back through compound alien eyes.

The viewpoint turned and shifted, distancing, moving away from the restless mosaic made up from the shattered remnants of ordinary life.

The effect was hypnotic. Josh had never seen anything like it. He sat trying to make sense of it, to piece it together. The more he stared, the more he realized that each segment had been chosen at random. It made no sense at all. Just as he got to grips with that, the camera began to zoom out and back. The little figures and small scenes were replaced by larger landscapes, cities, towns, villages, fields, rivers, lakes and mountains. Some like aerial camera shots, others more close up and specific: Manhattan skyscrapers, the Golden Gate Bridge, the 'Hollywood' sign, Everest.

The final view was from space as from an orbiting satellite. The Earth turned like a smashed glitter globe, revolving against the velvet black of space, dissolving into nothingness.

The camera now turned on to an interior of subdued lighting, satin-finished metallic surfaces, the subdued hum of machines.

'This must be the mothership. Most likely the end of it.'

But it was not the end of it. They were led through winding corridors into featureless rooms, shadowy interiors, surrounded by hovering entities, strapped to tables, fed down tubes, mind probed and measured, surrounded by scrambled screens and flashing, jumbled LEDs.

The place reminded him of somewhere. Somewhere he'd been recently. He frowned, trying to think where it was, but the memory eluded him. The other thing that struck him was the similarity to the accounts of alien abduction that he'd read.

'This place, these procedures,' he said without taking his eyes off the screen. 'They're like the missing time recalled under hypnosis by UFO abductees, experiencers.'

Katherine frowned. 'But that doesn't make sense!'

'How do you mean?'

'The game is called "HomeWorld", right? It's about an alien trying to get back?'

Josh nodded.

'So how come you get abducted? I mean,' she turned to him. 'Who are the aliens here?'

Josh did not have an answer for that. He turned back to the game, but every way he went now, they were trapped. Everything he tried brought them back to the same place. A white room with no windows. He flicked back and forth, face set and tense, getting angry, frustrated. Katherine put her hand on his, immobilizing the mouse.

'Save and shut down. We need to leave it.' She stretched her arms above her head to ease the tension in her neck.

'But we're no further on!'

'Perhaps we are, but we don't know it. Your mum's story and this.' She tapped the CD case. 'They are the same but told from different points of view.'

'I accept that. But I still don't see who—'

'Yes, you do. It has to be Patrick.'

'Not necessarily.'

'But you think it is.'

Joshua shifted uncomfortably. 'But Patrick's dead.'

'They've been lying. Your mum, your uncle, all of them.'

Joshua shook his head. He knew she was right. He just didn't want to believe it. 'But why would they do that?'

'That's what we have to find out. We need to know who wrote the game.'

'It should say in the manual somewhere.' Josh picked up the book, flicking through. 'Here we are: "Developed and designed by A. L. Ansom". That's the same name as the company. He must be the boss. What are you doing?'

Katherine was reaching for the phone. 'I'm going to ring them up. Find out exactly.'

'Alansom, Gina speaking.'

'Hi,' Katherine kicked in, bright and breezy, 'I wonder if you could help me? I want to contact Mr A. L. Ansom?'

'I'm afraid that person doesn't strictly exist,' the voice came back, polite but holding a hint of amusement. 'It's kind of like a pseudonym, you know? A pen name.'

'Oh, I see . . .'

Katherine was slightly put out, and was just about

to snap, I know what a pseudonym is, when Josh whispered, 'Ask her about the main designer.'

'In that case could I speak to the main designer of "AlienState 3", please?' Katherine shook her head, impatient with the reply she was getting. 'No, I don't want to be put through to the Hintline. There must be someone who was responsible for the original concept . . . OK, thanks. She's putting me through to another department,' she explained to Josh. 'Oh, hi . . .'

'Ask 'em . . .'

Katherine waved his whispered suggestions away impatiently and Josh had to be content just to listen as she ran through the spiel again. After a bit he gave up trying to interpret her 'I sees' and 'Unhuhs' and waited for her to finish.

'Umm, right. I see. Thanks very much.'

'What did he say?'

'Not much, really. The guy responsible for the game doesn't actually work there. Sounds like he's some kind of freelancer.'

'Can we find out where he lives?'

'No,' Katherine shook her head. 'They won't give out information like that. Anyway that guy was not even sure if he was still in the country. He's moving apparently.'

Katherine went over to the window. Joanna's car was back, parked in the drive. They had not heard it arrive. It could have been there for some time. She turned back to Josh. He was slumped forward, elbows on the table, head in his hands, unable to hide his disappointment.

'Come on,' Katherine shook him by the shoulder.

'Where are we going?'

'Next door. I think it's time we talked to your mother.'

# Chapter 22

Joanna Parker was in the dining room. The table was now tidy, the papers removed. The surface was clear of all but her computer, the printer, a stack of white paper. The computer was on. She was looking at the white screen, staring at the blinking cursor. She did not turn as Joshua and Katherine came in through the front door.

'Mum,' Josh said as he entered the room. 'There's a file in there called SUMMER.DOC. It's about when you were a kid, isn't it?'

She swung round to face him. Her face was blotched and streaked with mascara. She'd been crying.

'You've read it?' Joanna asked, her voice was distant and her look strange, as if she had been on a long journey and was only just coming back.

Josh nodded. 'I know I shouldn't have . . . I knew you'd be angry with me, but—'

'I'm not angry with you.' She shook her head slowly as if considering. 'Things have gone way beyond that.'

'The thing is Mrs Parker . . .' Katherine started.

'You've read it, too?' Joanna looked at the girl, eyes wide and then narrowing. She tensed, jaw clenched, as though bracing herself for yet more shocks.

'Well, yes . . . Don't blame Josh . . .'

'I don't blame him.'

Joanna looked from one to the other and back again, taking in Joshua's anguish and the girl's puzzlement. It was impossible to feel anger against them or resentment at their intrusion. They had begun to read the document in all innocence. How could they possibly have guessed at the dark secrets they would find within it?

'We've both read it, Mum,' Josh said quietly. 'And there's things we don't understand.'

'There's things I don't understand myself.'

Joanna turned away from them to gaze back at the screen. Her tone of resignation was almost more than Joshua could bear. He came up behind her, squeezing her shoulder. She groped for his hand, touching it to her cheek. When she looked up at him fresh tears threatened to spill.

'I think I'll go out in the garden for a bit. See if I can clear my head. While I'm there, you'd better read this.'

She reached for a sheaf of papers, neatly stacked by the printer, and handed them to her son.

## MISSING TIME

*I don't know how long we stayed like that, huddled together, listening to the rain on the leaves above us, beating out the end of our summer, and the end of our childhood. It could have been minutes, it could have been hours, but in that time many things changed and altered. We left the world of invention and make-believe. It was clear to us what had happened. The twins had followed Patrick. Or at least one of them had. William. He was always the most intrepid of*

182

*the two. He had dressed up in his alien outfit, intent on playing a trick on him. But the trick had gone terribly wrong. They were playing a game. We had all been playing a game in varying degrees. All except Patrick. To him it was reality.*

*We talked in fragments about what had happened, what we had seen, but our minds kept skidding away from the central thing. We felt responsible for Patrick. We were as much to blame as he was. We had as good as put the gun in his hand; we might as well have shot it ourselves. Paul confessed to me, there in the rustling semi-darkness beneath the trees, that he never saw the UFO. It was Patrick who saw it. Paul was convinced because he wanted to be, and Patrick never lied, did he?*

*'What did he see?' I whispered.*

*'I don't know, not exactly,' Paul hugged his knees to him. 'I've been thinking about it. I reckon it must have been some strange kind of weather trick. There was an electrical storm that night. Maybe lightning behind the clouds. And the neon from the new lights in town, they show a glow . . . What does it matter?' His voice had the dull, flat intonation of adult common sense. 'I took what he saw and twisted it and fed it back to him. I wanted so much for it to be a UFO . . .' He stood up wearily, pulling me with him. 'We'd better be getting back. Come on, Jo.'*

*We emerged to semi-darkness everywhere. Dusk was falling. The rain had not made the day any cooler. It was hotter, if anything, muggy and humid and there was a strange scorched smell in the air. The ground steamed. Wisps of mist rose from the drying earth, curling like smoke escaping from volcanic fumeroles.*

*We headed back across the fields, making for home. We had no idea what to do when we got there, or what to say.*

183

*We didn't know where Patrick was. We weren't even looking for him, but we found him anyway. He was in the flattened field of barley. The depressions in the crop no longer had their plaited appearance. I was looking with different eyes now. They were no longer mysterious, magical circles, but ragged patches beaten down by high winds. Patrick was standing stock-still right in the middle, just like the last time, head cocked at exactly the same angle, listening to the little insects. He held his arms out stiff; his hands fluttering, vibrating, just like wings.*

*He didn't notice us approaching. We were standing right in front of him and he didn't even look at us. Paul asked him what had happened at the pit behind Painter's Wood, but he didn't answer.*

*'What happened?' Paul asked again. 'What happened at the crash site, Patrick? You can tell us. It's OK.'*

*'No,' Patrick indicated the insects buzzing around us. 'They'll hear and relay the message. They'll tell the others where I am. I went to look for them. Then one of them came after me. I wanted to go with them, but he wanted to hurt me.' He put his hand to his head.*

*'Did you use this?' Paul took the gun out of the haversack and showed it to him.*

*'Yes,' Patrick nodded. 'I shot the gun. You can't trust the little flying saucer men. They mean us harm. They take people away and do bad things to them.' He indicated the insects flying everywhere. Ants were swarming, heavy, ungainly bodies under long grey wings. 'They are preparing to leave. They want to take me. I wanted to go before, but I don't think I do now. You won't let them take me, will you, Pauly?'*

*He looked at us, blue eyes pleading, through a blizzard of insects. We just stared back at him while the ants collected* on our clothes and in our hair, crawling over us. We were dumbfounded by him, by what he had done. A year before we would probably have made plans to run away, but something had happened to us. We had grown up. We had to take him home, face whatever music there was, but still we held back. He was our brother.

Eventually Paul said, 'We'd better get back.'

'Yes,' Patrick nodded. 'I was just thinking that myself.' Then he smiled. He didn't smile often, but when he did the effect was dazzling, like a young child.

Paul shouldered the haversack and Patrick came with no fuss, just followed along behind us, quiet and obedient. It was like taking a dog to be put down. It was almost dark by the time we got to our road. We were tired and dirty. I was so worried about what was going to happen to Patrick that I was beyond caring what Dad would do to us.

We came round the corner expecting the road to be deserted, but it was not. The whole street was out. All the neighbours: men in shirt sleeves, women in pinafores. There was Mrs Reynolds and her Robert, and Nigel and his mother, Ian with his mum and dad. I automatically looked for the twins. That was when it really punched home: they would never be together again. A feeling I struggle to name – guilt and fear mixed with horror, loss and sorrow – gripped me like seasickness. The reality of William's death came over me in waves.

The people in the street were subdued, standing in little knots, looking round every now and again, nodding and talking. The whole scene was infused with a brooding anxiety; the atmosphere was charged, electric with tension. It was as if they were waiting for something. Then I realized. They were waiting for us.

Ian saw us first. He was standing with his mum. He

tugged on her cardigan to alert her and then pulled back, like we had the plague. His mum grabbed him before he could say anything and dragged him away. I'll never forget the look on her face: horror and disgust all at once.

'Is that our Paul?' Mum came hurrying over. She grabbed Paul by the shoulder and shouted at him. 'Where's Patrick? Where is he?'

Paul did not say anything. Patrick's name was taken up by the crowd, repeated over and over, like a whispered mantra. They drew away from us, standing back as Patrick came through.

'Oh, thank God! Thank God!' Mum threw herself on him crying and sobbing. Patrick stood stiff in her embrace, hands at his sides. He stared round, his eyes beginning to slide about in panic. The situation was sufficiently out of the ordinary to frighten him, even though he didn't know what was going on.

We did.

Paul and I just looked at each other. It was to do with the twin. The one that was missing. We could see the police car outside the James's house.

Suddenly Dad was there. We thought he'd come to ask us what had happened, but he barged straight past, pushed Mum out of the way and began shaking Patrick, shouting: 'What have you done to him? What have you done?' Patrick went limp. He was flopping backwards and forwards like a puppet. Paul tried to get between them, but he was swatted away. Finally a policeman came over and forced Dad to let go.

'Do you know anything about this, son?' he asked. Paul nodded. 'Stay here.'

He left us and went up to the James's front door. The door was slightly ajar. The policeman pushed it open to call *his superior. Through the front windows I could see the James family sitting in a row on their settee, with Trevor in the middle. Then someone drew the curtains.*

*A big man came out of the house, not in uniform. He was tall, broad in the chest and shoulders, but not fat. His dark hair was Brylcreemed straight back.*

*'Where's your mum and dad?'*

*We looked around. They must have taken Patrick into the house.*

*'Where do you live?'*

*We pointed.*

*'Let's go.'*

*The crowd drew back, falling silent as we passed. I could feel them behind us, but all I could hear was my own heartbeat and the gravel crunching on our path. We stood on the porch. The door was shut. I listened to the familiar ring of the doorbell, and all the while I could feel the crowd seething behind me. I felt like a stranger outside my own house.*

*'Mr Jordan? Just a few questions.' The policeman stepped in, not waiting for Dad to invite him. 'Somewhere we can talk?'*

*Dad indicated the front room. We didn't use it very much. It smelt of coal fires and dust.*

*'You have another son?'*

*'Patrick.'*

*'Where is he?'*

*'He's upstairs. He's—'*

*'Can you bring him down, please?'*

*He nodded to his uniformed assistant to accompany Dad. Mum was hovering, twittering with nervous anxiety.*

*'Love a cup of tea, Mrs Jordan. Two sugars, and I like it nice and strong. Now then, you two . . .' He took Dad's*

187

*chair at the head of the dining room table and indicated for us to sit.*

From what he told us it wasn't difficult to work out what had happened. Trevor had come home that afternoon without his twin. They had been playing some kind of game, trailing Patrick. They had been following 'Indian File', one well behind the other. In our games, stalking was always done like that. Trevor had tracked them up to the new barbed-wire fence. At this point he heard dogs barking and was afraid that Farmer Harley had spotted them. He shouted for William to come back; but his twin either did not hear him, or ignored him. William was nearing the entrance to Painter's Wood by this time, still following Patrick. That was the last that Trevor saw of him. Farmer Harley had spotted him and was only one field away, shouting about what he did to trespassers, threatening to unleash his snarling dogs. This was too much for Trevor. He was caught out in the open. He would never make it up to Painter's Wood. If he went through the wire, he might end up in even more trouble. So he ran back home thinking that William would come back eventually. As afternoon turned to evening, and William was still missing, he told his mum, who told his dad when he got home from work.

'His dad called us. William still hasn't turned up.' The policeman stared across at us, head tilted back. His eyes were light blue, rimmed with black. 'We've got search parties out now looking for him. Can you shed any light on this matter?'

Paul and I looked at each other. We came to an agreement without a word being spoken.

'Yes, sir,' Paul spoke up.

'Truth now?' The light blue eyes narrowed.

'Of course, sir,' Paul said, sounding surprised. 'I wouldn't lie.'

And he didn't, but he only told pieces of the truth. Paul said nothing about the gun, even though it lay in the haversack next to his chair.

'Where did you last see William James?' The policeman took out a little black notebook bound by a thick elastic band.

'Out at Yarndale Common.'

The policeman looked up. 'You know it's dangerous there?'

Paul gulped and nodded.

'Was he with your brother?'

'Not exactly. William was following him, like Trevor said.'

'You were following?'

'Not exactly. Just went where they might be.'

'Why?'

'Why?' Paul looked at me. 'It was where we were going, going to play.'

'Play? You went there to play?' The policeman stopped writing in his little notebook. He stared as if he couldn't quite believe what Paul was saying. 'Didn't you see the warning signs?'

'Yes,' Paul's voice was barely audible. 'Yes, we did.'

'All right now,' he shut his eyes for a moment, as though he was tired. When he opened them again, they were bleak. It was as if he'd already seen what happened next. 'Take your time and tell me. Tell me exactly.'

'It, it was an accident. William was standing right on the edge of the crater, right on the edge of it. Then . . . then he must have lost his footing, or something and, and he, he tumbled down.'

189

'Tumbled down where?'

'Into the pit thing. We looked but we couldn't see him.'

'Where was Patrick?'

'He was climbing up.'

'Did he see what happened?'

'I, I don't know.'

'Why didn't you come home and say? Straightaway?'

'There, there was a terrible explosion. We,' he looked at me. 'We w-w-were f-f-frightened.' Memory made Paul gasp and stutter. He only just managed to get the sentence out.

'Where was Patrick?'

'He ran away.'

'And William?'

'We c-c-couldn't see him. He, he must of . . .' Paul shook his head. He had no words left.

'All right, son.' The policeman put down his pen and reached out his hand to him. 'It's all right. You did fine. It's up to us now.'

He stood up and went out into the hallway. There, he consulted the policeman who was talking to Patrick.

'Not the full shilling,' I heard the other one mutter. 'Can't get anything out of him. Won't say a word. Hang on a minute. Mr Jordan?'

All hell was breaking loose in the living room. Dad was yelling at Patrick, laying into him again. Mum began having hysterics, then she fainted. Mrs Reynolds came round to see to her.

The policemen left and while Mrs Reynolds looked after Mum downstairs, Paul crept up to Dad's room and put the gun back. We did not speak of it to each other. It was not a conscious decision, but we never told anyone about the gun. I guess we figured that Patrick was in enough trouble. They would not find out from him, either. The police quickly gave *up trying to question him. He would not speak to them. They questioned us instead, again and again, but we always told the same story until the truth became impossible. We could not tell them about the gun, not after we had left it out of every account.*

*Eventually the police accepted that it was an accident, but that was not enough to save Patrick. Despite what we'd said, and what the authorities believed, the rumours spread like poison. Beginning with Mr James, people heard 'Painter's Wood' and 'Patrick Jordan' and drew their own conclusions: 'Going off to the woods with a child so much younger . . . I told you he was never right . . . ' Before he'd been tolerated, seen as just a bit odd and eccentric. That all changed. His difference became twisted, turned into perversion. He was seen as a danger, to himself and other people. Only Mum tried to stick up for him, but with Dad against her, she didn't stand a chance.*

*It all got too much for her. She had a breakdown, I suppose we'd call it now. Then it was termed 'nervous exhaustion'. She was confined to bed, kept in a darkened room, sedated. Not to be disturbed. Not to be upset under any circumstances. She knew very little of what was going on at that time. Dad kept everything from her. We got to dread going up to see her; to be asked questions which we dared not answer.*

*The search for William went on; they went all through the motorway construction site, shifted tons of rock. They never found him. Over time, the whole episode became buried, but what with coming back here, and Mother so ill . . . At times like this, the past returns unbidden. It suddenly occurred to me, as I was driving up the motorway, he must be there still . . .*

Josh looked up from his reading, remembering their journey here, the near collision. The strange look on her face. They must have driven right over the place . . .

He got up and went into the garden to find his mother, to give her what comfort he could offer.

'What about Patrick? What happened to him, Mum?'

'Dad had him put away.'

'Put away where?'

'In a mental hospital.'

'But why? Didn't you try to stop him?'

'What could we do? We were children. No one takes any notice of children. We didn't know it was going to happen. He just went off in the car one morning and never came back. Dad kept it from Mum, she was still ill, but he told us. Paul and I . . . well, in a way, I suppose we thought that it was the best thing. After what happened with William, we knew we couldn't look after him anymore. We thought that he'd come home cured. Maybe not straightaway, but eventually. Meanwhile, we could visit. We packed his little suit-case full of stuff, ready to take to him, but then,' she stared down at her hands, twisting her wedding ring. 'Then Dad told us that he'd died. He said that Patrick had caught pneumonia, he'd always had a weak chest, and that it happened very suddenly. He'd gone down-hill very rapidly . . . And that's what I believed. Up until now.' She turned to face them, her grey eyes as bleak as a winter sea. 'Patrick's not dead, you see . . .'

Josh and Katherine exchanged looks. Joanna was confirming what they already suspected. Josh went to speak, but Katherine shook her head. His mother had things she had to say, and it was best not to interrupt her.

'That's what I've had to see the solicitor about. All the things I believed, all these years, they simply aren't true,' she paused, and when she went on her voice was dead-sounding, mechanical. 'I found these letters. In a drawer in Dad's desk. Going back years. Years and years. Letters about Patrick. They were from the hospital. St Chad's.'

'Where is that?' Josh asked.

'Not that far,' Katherine replied. 'It was the local, you know . . .'

'Loony bin,' Joanna supplied. 'And you're right. It's not far at all. He was there all the time. Just a few miles away and we never knew.' Joanna stopped and shook her head, unable to go on. 'I'm sorry. I'm so sorry . . .'

# Chapter 23

Joanna lapsed into silence. The sorrow she felt, the grief for a life gone by, was too great for words. All that missing time. Guilt and tears threatened to overwhelm her.

'But it's not your fault, Mum,' Josh got up from his chair, unable to bear the despair he saw on her face. 'How were you to know?'

He put his arm round her, patting her awkwardly, unsure what to do, looking to Katherine to come to the rescue.

'He's right, Mrs Parker,' Katherine nodded her agreement. 'Adults almost never tell you anything and they lie to you. They do. All the time. Especially if they feel guilty. It's like when my dad left. They kept telling me everything was brilliant and fine. Until he was walking out of the door. Then there's nothing you can do. It makes you feel like it was all your fault.' She stopped for a moment to reflect. 'I don't think they meant me to feel like that. They think they are protecting you, but the opposite is true. It leaves you so you can't face up to things. It leaves you feeling stupid and helpless.'

Joanna brushed away tears and looked at the girl.

'Call me Joanna, please.' She smiled ruefully. 'That's exactly how I feel now. Stupid and helpless.'

The smile made her looked young, vulnerable, more like them, somehow. The enamel coatings of adult life stripped away to reveal a child's pain and uncertainty.

'There must be something we can do,' Joshua said.

'The solicitor says he'll have to be traced. He said he'd look into it. They have people . . .'

'But it shouldn't be done by strangers!' Josh interrupted.

'So what are you suggesting?'

'We should do it. We're his family. We should have a go, at least. It's better to do something. Act. You always say that.'

'I know, but . . .' Joanna cut off the objections that sprang into her head, fully fledged. She had to get her mind out of shutdown mode. She had to release the reservoir of silence that had slowly poisoned her family life. 'Yes,' she said, instead. 'Yes.'

The word felt good in her mouth, just saying it made her feel stronger. She began to lose that hunted frightened look. The life came back into her eyes.

'Yes. You're right. Let's do it. Where do we start?' She looked to her son now. These were early days. She would need Joshua's optimism and energy, his untainted strength, if she was to escape this house of secrets.

'First of all,' Joshua hesitated, unused to being deferred to, suddenly nervous in case he blew it. 'Well, first of all,' he said again but section by section, his mind was going blank, throwing him into a panic.

'The letters,' Katherine prompted.

'Oh, yes,' Josh grinned his thanks. 'What about

where they came from? Couldn't we contact the hospital?'

Joanna shook her head. 'I thought of that. St Chad's was closed years ago. Converted into flats.'

'Where are the letters?' Joshua asked. 'Can I see them?'

'Sure. They're here.' Joanna opened her bag and took out a bundle secured with elastic. 'The last ones are from a psychiatrist, asking for childhood details. But they are all written from the hospital.'

Josh took them from her anyway, and began sorting through them.

'There's always the game,' Katherine said after a moment or two.

Mother and son looked at her. Their eyes were exactly the same shade of grey.

'Game? What game?' Joanna frowned.

' "AlienState 3",' Josh supplied. 'The one you bought me. We've been playing it.'

'What's it got to do with this?'

'It's very like your story,' he explained, going through the points of similarity.

'It's more than "like",' Katherine insisted. 'We're talking identical events seen from different points of view. You didn't write it, did you?'

'I couldn't even play one, let alone write it.'

'So who?' Katherine looked at her, head tilted on one side.

'The person who wrote it,' Joanna's eyes widened. 'You think it could be Patrick?'

'Yes,' Katherine glanced at Josh. 'We do.'

'Show me.'

*

196

Joanna sat transfixed, only her eyes moving, taking in one scene after another, as her son took her through the game. It finished at the same point as before. The girl was right, it was uncanny. Joanna sat for a moment, not saying anything, staring at the screen, trying to think.

'Could we phone and find out who wrote it?'

'We already tried,' Josh shook his head. 'No dice.'

'That was us,' Katherine pointed out. 'It might be different for your mum.'

It wasn't different for Joanna. She got the same non-committal response that Katherine had before.

'He's very reclusive, apparently. Absolutely no contact. They won't even give his name out.' She slumped at the table, swamped by a backwash of disappointment. 'What do we do now?'

'I've been thinking,' Josh fanned the letters in front of him. 'When did these stop?' He picked up the last one. 'When Grandpa died?'

His mother nodded.

'What if there's more?'

'How do you mean?'

'They wouldn't just stop, would they? The sender,' he read the name from the end of the letter, 'this Dr E. Campbell, wouldn't know to stop because Grandpa was dead. The letters would carry on.'

'Which Gran would get and might have kept! Well done, Josh!' Joanna stood up and hugged her son, making him blush. 'You're a genius!'

Katherine grinned and said, 'Good thinking, Boy Wonder.'

'She might have chucked them out.' Joanna let go of him, her face clouding with doubt.

'And she might not, Mum,' Josh looked at her sternly. 'It's no good being negative like that. Did Gran have any special place where she kept things?'

'There used to be a tin, in the kitchen cupboard. A biscuit tin. But that was years and years ago, surely not now?'

'Why not? She was a creature of habit, you said so yourself.' Josh stood up. 'Come on, it's worth having a look.'

'What type of biscuit?' Josh jumped on a stool and began rummaging through the top shelf of the kitchen cupboard.

'Huntley and Palmer's.'

'Bingo.'

Josh parted the dry goods and pulled the rusty tin from the back of the cupboard. It contained a bewildering mix of things, buttons, unpicked zips, corn plasters, pension books, a sum of paper money and a bundle of letters, bound by a rubber band. These were different from the others. These had been opened and read.

# Chapter 24

The first letters were on hospital notepaper.

7th January,1992

*Dear Mrs Jordan,*

*Forgive my delay in responding to your letter. After so many years your reply rather stunned me. I understand now the reason for all these years of silence. Please accept my condolences, and also Patrick's. One of the advantages of his condition is that he bears no grudges.*

*I'm sure that you will be glad to know that he continues well and that he is responding very positively to his present regime of treatment. You do not mention it in your letter, but we (Patrick and I) have discussed the possibility of meeting with you. He is quite willing and happy for me to arrange this, if it is agreeable to you.*

*Please let me know if you would like this to go ahead. Meanwhile thank you again for making contact and showing your concern. Even after all this time, it is important for Patrick to know that there are people who care for him.*

*I wonder if I could ask you to fill in this questionnaire? It relates to Patrick's early life and your responses might help me understand more about him and would help a great deal in deciding the future course of his treatment. I have requested this before but have never received any response – for obvious reasons.*

*I promise to keep you up to date.*

*yours,*

*E. Campbell*

*20th February, 1992*

*Dear Mrs Jordan,*

*Thank you once again for your letter and for returning the questionnaire so promptly. Your answers will be a great help. I have been studying them eagerly and they do provide valuable insights into my patient, this in turn should help to find the best treatment for him. Patrick's rehabilitation is slow work, and we still have good days and bad, but the good days can stretch into weeks. Patrick has many talents and interests which more than compensate for any on-going problems he might have. It is only a matter of time before he finds the right outlet. I'm sure you know and understand that your son is a truly exceptional person.*

*I do not know how much you know about Patrick's disorder. He has Aspergers Syndrome, you might be more familiar with the term Autism. He has difficulty relating to and socially interacting with other people. I can see from your responses to my questionnaire that as a child he exhibited many of the features associated with these types of disorders. Nothing can make up for the years of misdiagnosis and neglect that Patrick suffered, and there is no specific treatment, or cure, but we have put together a package of interventions and Patrick's response has been phenomenal. He is blessed with very high ability and I'm sure that someday soon all his hard work will be rewarded.*

*I am sorry that you do not wish to meet Patrick, but I quite understand your reasons and rest assured that he does too. Privately I think it was rather a relief for him! Perhaps you know him better than I do!*

*Although you do not want contact to extend as far as meeting, I will take the liberty of keeping in touch. I hope this is acceptable to you.*

*yours,*

*E. Campbell*

The correspondence which followed had been irregular. Christmas cards and a couple of letters a year containing updates on Patrick's welfare and treatment, chronicling the changes in him and his circumstances.

*March, 1993*
*You are right. The hospital is due to close soon, but*
*that does not pose a problem for either of us. Patrick's*
*rehabilitation is complete, or as complete as it will*
*ever be. He has been living independently for some*
*time now and no longer needs the kind of support an*
*institution like that provides. I am taking retirement,*
*it seems like the most appropriate time! I'll keep you*
*posted on how we're doing. Meanwhile, all the best.*

*December, 1994*
*How time flies. Turn around and it's Christmas! I*
*miss the snow – I'm from New York, you know. We*
*are getting along just fine. I'm kept busy with my*
*research and my private patients. Patrick has finally*
*decided to take up my offer and move into my place.*
*It's plenty big enough for the both of us.*

*July, 1995*
*We have exciting news. Patrick has finally found the*
*outlet that he has been looking for. He met a man*
*at a UFO Conference (he is still fascinated by all that*
*stuff) and they got talking. It seems this man works*
*in a software company, but is looking to set up on his*
*own. He liked some of Patrick's ideas. So fingers*
*crossed.*

*December, 1996*
*Here we are again! (Oh, I think I said that last year.)*
*Glad to know you're keeping well. Patrick's*
*involvement in the company I told you about is*
*growing. I worried at the start that it would be too*
*much for him. He's proved me wrong again! He's*

*thriving! Your son never ceases to amaze me. He'd
make you proud, believe me.*

*December, 1997*
*Season's Greetings. I hope this letter finds you well.
We're both just fine. Patrick has been very busy this
year, but he copes well as long as he's left alone to
work at his own pace. Generally it's OK, Alan (who
co-owns the company) knows he can't be pressured.
He deals with most things, leaving Patrick free to do
what he does best. The company they started has
grown out of all recognition! They are talking stock
market flotation! It started with a couple of guys in a
little place over a shop, now their offices are state of
the art. Not that Patrick ever goes there. He prefers to
work from home, but it is his games that have made
them.*

*November, 1998*
*Alansom – Patrick's company – are set to be taken
over. How this will affect us, I don't know. Patrick's
not interested in big outfits and he's not interested in
money. He liked it when it was small (more fun then
– he says) So I sense big changes on the way. Don't
worry – I'll keep you posted.*

'We've got him,' Josh breathed. 'He's the man.'

'Looks like it,' Katherine nodded.

The last letter curled in Josh's hand as a fierce rush
of triumph surged through him. But it was more than
being proved right, finding the answer, solving the
mystery. He felt a kind of awe that was hard to explain

to anyone who didn't play games. His own uncle had designed the 'AlienState'. He couldn't believe it.

'Are there any more in there?'

Katherine shook her head. 'Hang on, though. Take a look at this.' She dug around, extracting another envelope from right at the bottom of the biscuit tin.

This one was different from the others, smaller, more frail, and pale violet, not cream or white. There was no name on the front, no address, no indication of what it might contain. The flap was not fixed. Katherine tipped the contents out on to the table. A photograph and a lock of hair, baby fine and fair, tied with faded blue thread.

'Let me see.' Josh's heart beat hard and his hand almost trembled as he took the photograph from her and gazed into the face of his lost uncle.

The image had been cut from the end of a group picture. Josh knew the one. It was on Gran's bureau upstairs. The composition was off centre, lopsided, he had always thought there was something strange about it. Now he knew why. He went up to Gran's room and brought it down, pulling the photo out of the frame. The mounting had hidden the cut edge.

He was standing next to Paul, but slightly apart, a small but carefully defined space between him and his brother. Everyone else was watching the birdie, but Patrick was staring off to the side, face turned away from the camera. Josh judged him to be about eleven or twelve, but he had been tall for his age. Paul, dark and stocky by his side, hardly reached his shoulder. He was wearing formal clothes for a kid even then, long trousers, jacket and tie. His fair hair flopped long into his eyes. The picture was black and white, but

Josh could tell the eyes were blue. The gaze was far away as though he was expecting something interesting to happen off in the distance. He held his hands high in front of his chest clutching each other as if for comfort. His face was creased, his lips pulled back, less of a smile, more an expression of agony.

'I remember when that was taken.' His mother took the two pieces and laid them down on the table. 'On the front at Torquay. A man came along taking snaps. Patrick didn't like having his photo taken, I guess it shows. Mum was so pleased, it was the only one with us all together.'

'So what happened?' Katherine asked. 'Who cut it up?'

'My dad. After Patrick.' She had to stop and search for the right words. 'After he went away, Dad went all through the house removing everything that belonged to Patrick, every reminder of him. It was all burned. All except the stuff Paul and I had collected together and put in his little case. Paul hid it.'

'I found it.' Josh said quietly.

'Did you? When?'

'Not long after we first got here.'

'Why didn't you say anything?'

'I don't know,' Josh looked away. 'I thought you'd be angry.'

The prohibition on Patrick had even affected his generation. Joanna put up a hand to her brow to massage away the pain. The aching sorrow had come back again, it was lodged in her head like a migraine.

'We were forbidden to refer to him, or ever speak of him,' she said eventually. 'He effectively became a non-person. It was as if he had never existed.'

'But why? Why would anyone do such an awful thing?'

'Why would anyone lie and pretend that someone had died? You would have to know my father to understand. At the time he said he was doing it to protect Mum, so she wouldn't take on. She had a kind of breakdown, like I said. Nothing could be done to upset her. And that's how it stayed. No one allowed to even say his name. Until now.'

She stopped speaking and stared down at the table, moving the two fragments of photograph with her fingers, matching the cut edges together, re-uniting Patrick with the rest of his family.

'I found this, too.' Josh handed a cream envelope to his mother. 'It was up in the letter rack in Gran's room.'

It was unopened. Maybe Mrs Reynolds had popped it in the rack, ready for Gran to read when she came back from hospital. Joanna cut through the flap with a knife and they all crowded round to read the contents. The home address was the same as on the letters from the tin box: Broome Cottage, Easthough, a small village on the other side of the county. It was dated June of this year, just after Gran had her second stroke.

*Dear Mrs Jordan,*

*Patrick and I have puzzled over your long silence and we both hope that all is well. I meant to write you before, but the last few months have been very busy. Patrick and I are re-locating to the States, to California. Patrick has sold his interest in the*

*company, and has been invited to work with the kind
of small outfit which suits him best. He is very keen
to go. I have agreed to accompany him as, now that
I'm retired, there is little to keep me here in the UK.*

*I think the move will be good for the both of us.
Patrick especially. He already has many, many
friends there via the Internet and there is a great deal
of support and understanding Stateside for people
with his condition.*

*I will send you our new address, when we have one!*

*Patrick sends his regards.*

*Yours, as ever,*

Joanna smoothed the letter flat and laid it down with
the others. She stood for a moment, staring down at
them, thinking about the astonishing story that they
told. She was amazed and glad, glad that Patrick had
overcome all the forces set against him. Not only that,
but he had found an outlet for his extraordinary
talents, which had been quite exceptional, even when
he was a child. She wondered about this Dr E.
Campbell, and thought that she'd like to meet him,
or her, it could be a her. And she wondered about her
mother. The effect of that first letter must have been
seismic, rocking her life like an earthquake, and yet
she said nothing. Not to her daughter, not to Paul,
not to Mrs Reynolds next door. She preferred to keep
quiet about it, keep it secret. The habits of a lifetime
are hard to change.

'We know where he lives,' Joshua waved the last letter. 'We can find him.'

'Oh, Josh . . . I don't know . . .'

Joanna bit her lip. What had Paul said about stirring it all up again? Patrick sounded happy, settled. She did not want to come back into his life trailing guilt and its consequences like some ghastly apparition forty years dead.

'We have to, Mum,' Josh insisted, sensing her faltering resolve. 'We've got this far. We can't go back now.'

# Chapter 25

'Hello,' Patrick rose to welcome them. 'You must be my sister, Joanna.' He came forward to shake her hand. 'And you must be Joshua. My nephew. You look a lot like my brother, Paul.'

Josh shook hands shyly. The fingers grasping his felt smooth and cool. The grip was firm but brief.

'Edie has told me all about your visit. I'm very pleased. Pleased to meet both of you.'

'I am, too. After all this time. It's . . .' Joanna shook her head. 'I can't explain.'

'You don't have to. Come and sit down.'

He was a tall man, and very thin, dressed in jeans and camel work boots. His face was pale, as though he spent little time outdoors. Blue eyes, the shade of his soft denim shirt, darted from side to side before focusing back on his guests. He ran a long thin hand over grey hair cropped close to his head.

'Can I get you something? Coffee? Tea?' He asked once they were seated.

'Edie's bringing some over,' Joanna said.

'Good. She's better at those things than me. I'm not very domesticated. I always forget people take things like sugar.'

Edie came in and put the tea things on the table

and then withdrew. Patrick busied himself pouring, his movements deft and neat. While he served them, he asked about his mother, accepting news of her death with a little jerking shake of the head. He asked after Paul, and then the rest of the family, his nephews and niece that he had never seen. His manner was polite, pleasant, but the questions, and the way he asked them, gave Josh the impression that he was acting a part, working from a pre-rehearsed script.

They sipped their tea and Joanna did her best to answer, to fill in the acres of time missing for him, but he seemed to be scarcely listening. He had his next enquiry ready before her last response was finished. Every now and then his hand went to his throat, twisting some kind of talisman he wore there fastened by a short leather thong.

'A gift from a friend. A Navaho,' he said suddenly, cutting across Joanna, noting Joshua's interest. 'When I'm nervous I fiddle with things. He gave me this to remind me. He lives out in the desert. Not far from Dreamland. Area 51.' He read Joanna's puzzled look. 'Where the US government keep all their secrets. You know, don't you?'

Josh nodded.

'Do you believe?'

'I want to.'

'That's good.'

'Do you?' Josh asked him. 'Believe in aliens, I mean?'

Patrick thought for a moment. 'Some of my friends think that they are already here.'

Josh laughed, thinking he was joking. Patrick didn't laugh back. The conversation came to a halt after that.

Josh and his mother looked at each other. Patrick seemed perfectly at ease. If the silence between them was awkward, he had not noticed. Joshua sat still, trying to think of something to say, but his eyes kept straying to the wall at the end of the long room.

The whole length was one big work station. Pin boards behind and to the sides were covered in huge designs, colour printouts, textured bit maps, ink drawings, pencil sketches.

'I have to check my e-mail.' Patrick stood up and went over to the computer. 'I have many on-line friends. Some I have met through my interest in UFOs, some through games and gaming, although that's work, really. Some because I have an autistic spectrum disorder.'

It was not a challenge, or to evoke sympathy. It was a statement of fact. Head to one side, he looked at Joanna. It was the first time she recognized this man as her brother.

'Here, see.' He beckoned Josh over and began typing. 'These are some of my on-line buddies.' A list of names scrolled up the side of the screen. 'Do you want to be one?'

Josh nodded.

'Good. That's good. I'll give you my e-mail address. We can keep in touch then.' He turned round to look at mother and son. 'I communicate better that way. I don't have to worry about faces and voices, which makes it easier for me.'

'What's all that?' Josh pointed to the wall in front of him.

'It's a new game I'm designing. That's what I do.'

He held his head on one side again. 'But I guess Edie told you that, too.'

'I already knew.' Josh mumbled.

'Say again?'

'I already knew,' Josh repeated, this time more loudly. 'You did the "AlienState" series. Katherine, she's a friend of mine,' he explained quickly, 'Katherine and I played the last one, "HomeWorld". Well, some of it, and because it was so like the stuff Mum was writing, we worked out it was you. Well, not entirely, but we thought it must be. We even tried to phone you at your company but they wouldn't put us through.'

'Alansom?'

Josh nodded.

'I founded the company with Alan, he's the chairman. Edie lent me the money. It was quite a coincidence. My middle name is Alan.'

'I know,' Josh said. 'Mine is, too.'

'Another coincidence!' Patrick exclaimed. 'I'm interested in coincidences.'

'It's not really,' Josh said, shyly. 'I think Mum named me after you.'

'Did she? How,' he frowned, groping for a word. 'Curious. Anyway, "Alansomeone" it was to be. I was the someone. Alan said it was too long, so we cut it to Alansom. We then invented the person, A. L. Ansom. That was me.' Patrick laughed, a slow rippling chuckle. ' "HomeWorld" is the last "AlienState". There won't be any more. I wrote it as a personal memoir. And you recognized it? How extraordinary. You write?'

Patrick swung in his chair, turning back to Joanna.

212

'Well, yes . . .'

'What kind of things?'

'Novels and stories. For children. I was writing about us, our childhood. It's sort of autobiographical, not meant for publication,' she added quickly. 'Josh read it.'

'Do you write science fiction?' he asked, twisting the conversation in another unexpected direction.

'Er, no,' Joanna shook her head. 'I don't.'

'I love science fiction. And fantasy.' His long hands folded over each other. 'I have done since I was a boy. I've got a great collection.' He turned to Josh. 'Do you like science fiction?'

'Yes.'

'I'll show you. You can borrow some. But first the game. Do you want to see what I'm working on?'

Josh nodded again.

'Sit next to me.' He closed his e-mail file and brought up a different programme. 'This is not like the "AlienState" series. This is more myth and fantasy. "AlienState" is about being isolated in a world that's hostile.' As he spoke he punched up different environments and landscapes, some of them truly magical. Josh sat in awe. Hardly anyone had seen these before. 'This is more like exploring a world which is neither good nor bad. It sounds boring but it won't be.' He swung round on his chair to face his nephew. 'Do you want to help design a little bit of it?'

'*Do* I?'

'That's what I asked,' Patrick folded his arms nodding to the touch screen in front of him. 'Do you want to design a bit of it?'

'Yes,' Josh replied quietly. 'That would be nice.'

Talking to Uncle Patrick was not quite like talking to any other person, but he was beginning to get used to it. Like Mum said, it wasn't that hard if you allowed yourself to follow in the tracks of his mind.

Joanna let herself out quietly and went to find Edie.

Patrick lived in a row of converted outhouses, entirely separate from the main house. Joanna stepped into strong sunlight and crossed the paved courtyard to a long low stone building. The back door was open into the kitchen. The downstairs rooms were empty. She called up into the house, but got no reply.

She eventually found Edie in the back garden. This was immaculately set out, with a long clipped lawn flanked by formal borders.

'Patrick likes to garden,' Edie commented as they strolled past tall plants, red hot pokers and hollyhocks, standing to attention behind rows of smaller bedding plants set out in alternating colours. 'But the result can be kind of regimental.'

Joanna laughed, 'It reminds me of my father. He had tulips marching all round the garden in lines of four exactly a foot apart. They looked like miniature soldiers on parade.'

'Really?' Edie's greeny grey eyes sharpened behind her glasses. 'Autism, or more correctly Aspergers Syndrome in Patrick's case, often runs in families, you know. It's quite common for a patient's father, or mother, or grandparents even, to have exhibited the same kind of behaviours, which were seen at the time as just being rather eccentric. I'd like to know more about him.' Edie Campbell pushed back her mass of iron grey curls and smiled. 'There I go again, talking like a psychiatrist.'

Edie's strong face, tanned and hardly lined, made her look young for her age. She had only recently given up her clinical work but Joanna judged her to be well over 60. She glanced in and waved through the leaded squares of Patrick's window but the two heads were bent towards the computer screen. Josh glanced up for a moment, his unfocused gaze flicking from her to the garden, then he looked down again. Joanna turned back to her companion, asking about her career. What had kept her in Britain.

'Why stay and work for the NHS? Too stubborn to go home, I guess.'

Her easy charm and wry sense of humour served to disguise a deep and abiding compassion for the mentally ill. She was truly Patrick's saviour. She had found him languishing on the back wards, dismissed as a hopeless case: misdiagnosed as schizophrenic, pumped with enough drugs to fell an elephant, thoroughly institutionalized, permanently sedated.

'I was the first one to notice there was someone home,' she said simply.

She had devoted herself to coaxing him back into life. Not only that, she had discovered within him a remarkable human being.

'Talent like that shouldn't be wasted. Don't look for a cure,' she added as they sat in the shade of a pair of apple trees. 'Patrick's lucky in that he's at the higher functioning end of the spectrum, but there is no cure for autism. The key is not to think that way. Just accept that it's part of who he is. The disorder has a positive as well as a negative side. I'm not underestimating the problems, these are truly formidable, to us almost unimaginably so. But I don't think we should ignore the positive aspects either. Without it he'd be just an average Joe. It's his other powers that make him different. His concentration of thought, single-mindedness, the way he sees the world, these things make him truly exceptional.' She leant forward, fixing Joanna with an intensity born of deep conviction. 'Think of all the pleasure he gives to kids like Josh, and not just kids. Plenty of adults enjoy his games, too. Including psychiatrists. The "AlienState" series? It's like a route map into what it is like to be autistic. It's his way of increasing awareness. How much do you know about his condition?'

'Not a lot. I've read some books . . .'

'There's all kinds of theories as to what causes it, everything from brain abnormality to hormone deficiency.' She shook her head. 'It's a truly baffling disability. Because we don't understand, it is very easy for us to dismiss autistics as limited, simply because they are not like us. Their abilities are seen as "odd anomalies", "of no consequence". I used to be like that, finding ways to explain the inexplicable, finding ways to downgrade astonishing feats of savant ability. Did you know that there are people who can tell you on what day of the week a date will fall way into the next millennium? Or hold in their heads a three hundred figure digit? Or tell you precisely how many peas you've spilled on the floor? Who can memorize pages at a glance and recite them back to you weeks afterwards? Draw the whole of a building after just one look at it? Idiot Savants – that's what they get called. Note the "idiot". These powers are dismissed as isolated oases in a desert of disability. Well, maybe. Patrick has taught me to see differently. I sometimes think it's us who can't understand. Innocents, the Russians used to call them, Holy Innocents, and they were valued as such. They have much to teach us. I sometimes think we ignore autistic talent because we are jealous . . .' She smiled and turned to her companion. 'I guess I'm rattling on, I am sorry. Do feel free to stop me.'

'Not at all! It's fascinating . . . I'm just so glad you found him,' Joanna paused, trying to find the words to express her gratitude. 'You've done so much for him. I can't begin . . .'

Edie dismissed Joanna's stumbling thanks with a shake of her head. 'It's a long row to hoe, and a hard one, and we're not there yet. Sure, Patrick's come a long way, and that's down to him, not me. His determination, his ability. Things a four-year-old child takes for granted, knows instinctively, he has to figure out. He has to compute other people's states of mind, their intentions. To do this, he has to learn, and keep on file ready for instant recall, a vast bank of facial expressions, gestures, turns of phrase, tones of voice, all the things that tell us how another person is feeling, what they are thinking. Similarly, he does not feel and think the way we would, particularly in social situations, so his natural behaviour would seem bizarre. He's had to learn to act, learn the rules and obey them. "Normal" doesn't come naturally, and it doesn't come easy.'

Joanna couldn't reply. Tears welled and spilled from her eyes. The thought of her brother, locked up and neglected, left for dead for all those years, was more than she could bear.

'You mustn't blame yourself, my dear,' the psychiatrist leaned over and squeezed her shoulder. 'You were just a child. Patrick certainly doesn't. It is the odd nature of his affliction; it can be a blessing as well as a curse. Look at it like this: in some ways he's a stranger to the kind of love and affection we take as a given right, but hatred, bitterness, resentment leave him unmarked.'

'There are things, things that happened, that Patrick did . . .' Joanna let out a shuddering sigh. 'Paul and I, we never said—'

'You mean with William James, the twin who disappeared?'

'You know about it?'

'I did a little research. The incident was referred to in Patrick's hospital notes. I'd like you to tell me what you saw.'

Joanna told her what had happened out at the pit, reliving it, going through it all again, bit by bit.

'You saw a gun go off. You saw a child fall. But you two, you and Paul, weren't the only ones there, and you weren't up close. Patrick was there, too. He has a most powerful memory, as many autistic people do. He has exact recall. It is what allows him to create his games in such detail. He can describe that afternoon, even down to individual sounds and fleeting scents. It's clear from what he has told me that he *was* very frightened and he *did* think he was being attacked. But although he *did* have the gun, and it *did* go off, the child had begun to fall even before he shot. The bullets missed him. He was already slipping out of Patrick's line of vision.'

'Why didn't he say anything?'

'You know the answer to that yourself. He could not understand what was happening around him. He withdrew, retreated into his citadel.'

'All these years I thought—'

Joanna felt her cheeks flame. Tears threatened again. She had thought him guilty, just like everybody else.

'We tried to find William's family, to tell them what happened. Patrick thought he owed it to them, thought they should know.'

'Did you find them?'

Edie shook her head. 'His parents are both dead. The other twin, Trevor, we traced as far as Australia, but then the trail petered out. We did our best.' She turned to Joanna. 'Patrick has put the incident behind him. It happened to a younger self, not who he is now. I suggest you learn from him and try and do the same thing.'

'Joanna?' Patrick asked just before they were leaving. 'I would like to read the autobiographical piece when it is finished.'

Joanna smiled as she remembered an important thing about him. Even when he did not appear to be listening he was in fact taking everything in.

'Of course. I'll send you a copy.'

'Thank you. Thank you very much. We will keep in touch via the Internet. Josh is helping me to design a game.'

'I'm not really . . .' Josh blushed.

'I thought you were,' Patrick frowned. 'Does that mean you don't want to do it any more?'

'Oh, no,' Josh shook his head vigorously, blushing even more. 'I just meant I wouldn't be any good, that's all.'

'Oh, I see,' Patrick's face cleared. 'I understand now. False modesty.' He turned to Joanna. 'What about Paul? I would like to see him before I go to America. Do you think something could be arranged?'

'I'm sure . . .' Joanna hesitated. 'But he's not how you remember.'

'Don't worry, Joanna,' Patrick smiled for the first time. 'Nothing is.'

# Chapter 26

'How was it?' Katherine asked when Joshua got back.

'Brilliant.'

'What's your uncle like?'

'He's great. Nothing like other adults. He's interested in the same things as me. You know, aliens and UFOs. He's got a great comic collection and you should see his computer system. Real cutting edge—'

'How did your mum get on? I mean seeing him again, it must have been difficult.'

'Yes, it was quite a strain, I guess, particularly to begin with. All the way there she was really tense, but it got easier once they'd met. I think she found it all rather upsetting, but in a good way, you know? She's glad she went, anyhow. She seems really relieved, like a big weight is off her shoulders. She couldn't stop talking on the way home. She's telling Uncle Paul about it now on the phone. Hey,' he added after a moment. 'We were right. Alansom? That's him. And, guess what?'

Katherine shook her head. 'Couldn't possibly.'

'He wants me to design a game with him.'

'Really?' Katherine's eyebrow arched. 'A treat for games fans everywhere. The community waits with bated breath.'

'I knew you'd take the—'

'I'm not. Honestly.' She grinned, linking arms with him. 'Don't sulk, it spoils your looks. Speaking of games, I've got something important to show you.'

'What?'

'Come with me.'

'Yesterday, while you were away, I got to the end of the game. Want to see?'

'How did you do that?'

'I could say I slaved all day using all my puzzle-solving powers and superior mental ability. I could say that. On the other hand I could have phoned the Hintline and chatted up the bloke. I told him I wanted to impress my boyfriend.' Katherine laughed and winked at him. 'He was surprisingly helpful.'

'What? You aren't supposed to do that!'

Josh tried to ignore her teasing, though he felt the heat rising up the back of his neck. Among his friends getting help of any kind was regarded as serious cheating.

'Don't be silly! How are you supposed to get to the end otherwise? It could take days! Weeks.'

'But that's the whole point!' Josh made a small whimpering sound and clutched at the hair on the sides of his head.

'Maybe, in the ordinary way of things,' Katherine conceded, 'but we haven't got time for that. Now pay attention.'

The game's Hintline guy had obviously instructed her well. By using various code combinations and manipulating the operating system Katherine short cut her way right to the last stage of the game.

'The White Room rotates, which shows that, voilà! One wall is a mirror. Which you then have to smash! Like that!'

The effect was startling and immediate. The wall shattered into hundreds of tumbling shards of flying glass. An illusion of such power and intensity that Josh jumped back, thinking that the screen had imploded. Each jagged sliver moved in silent slow motion holding different parts of one picture. Gradually they settled, coalescing to show an Earth-like planet, magical blue and green under icing swirls of creamy white cloud. The image held, floating in the vastness of space, before the camera plummeted, arrowing down in a heart-stopping freefall.

Clouds sped past on both sides and then parachutes popped, braking the descent to drifting slowness. Under the cloud cover lay a familiar landscape of green fields and woodlands, snaked over by rivers and cut across by roads.

The fall grew faster and faster; the ground rushing up to meet the camera. Then suddenly it all finished.

A grid pattern filled the screen again, like at the beginning of the game.

'Now.' Katherine used the mouse to wipe the blackness away with a side to side flick of the wrist. It was like cleaning a window, which was exactly right, because that is what the squares were. Just like at the beginning, but this time looking out, not in. Josh peered through the clearing screen. The scene was familiar to him. Jewel-like flowers studded the borders of a long expanse of green running down to apple trees.

'It's Patrick's garden,' he breathed.

'Welcome to "HomeWorld",' a quiet voice said back to him. 'Congratulations on arriving safely.'

# Chapter 27

'I'm going to miss you!' Katherine put an arm round Joshua and hugged him to her.

'No, you're not!' Josh pulled away.

'I am! I am, really. Don't look so miserable. What's the matter?'

Josh didn't know what to say. At one time he'd wanted to go home more than anything in the world, now with the car packed and ready to go, he wanted to stay.

He looked up at the house. Uncle Paul had come at the weekend to help Mum clear out all the stuff. It had taken a couple of days, a skip, and many trips to the tip. Each night they had a takeaway, and Mum and Paul stayed up late, talking into the night. Josh did not know what they said. He did not eavesdrop. He went to bed and left them to it, but each morning they seemed happier, more at ease with themselves and each other.

Uncle Paul had gone and the house was empty now. Empty of all its furniture, empty of all the bits and pieces and bric-a-brac. Each room swept clean. Nothing left of the people who had lived there or their secrets. The 'For Sale' sign was up in the front garden. It was waiting now for another family. Josh wondered what their lives would be, whether they had a secret history. Once they moved in, there would be no call to come back anymore. If he was going to ask, he'd better do it now.

'Before I go,' he said, turning back to her, 'there's one thing I want to know.'

'Go ahead. Shoot.'

'Anything?'

'Anything. Absolutely.'

'Well . . . I was wondering, just wondering, if I was older, say sixteen, or seventeen, Barry's age say . . .'

'Ye-es,' Katherine nodded, 'if you were Barry's age, I'm with you so far.'

'Well, I was wondering, just wondering . . .'

'As you said.'

'As I said. I was wondering if, if you'd go out with me. If, if, that was the case . . . Don't laugh!'

Josh looked stricken as Katherine's straight-faced expression broke apart.

'I'm not laughing, not at you, not directly.' She looked away, trying to compose herself, and when she looked back her face was still full of humour, but her green-flecked hazel eyes were soft, luminous – whether with tears or laughter, it was hard to tell. 'You are the sweetest boy I've ever met,' she said simply. 'But would I go out with you?' She looked at him, forefinger on chin, pretending to think. 'Hmm, well . . . that would depend.'

'On what?'

'What you looked like, of course. Now, go on.' She nodded towards the house. Joanna was closing the front door. 'Your mum's ready to go.'

'Keep in touch?'

226

'Of course.'

Mrs Reynolds joined Katherine to wave them off. Josh twisted in his seat, keeping his eyes on the girl until the turn in the road obscured her from view. He settled back in his seat, wondering whether she would keep in touch or not. On balance he thought that she probably would. Katherine was the kind of girl who kept her word and, in a strange kind of way, they had been through a lot together.

He did not say much on the way home, neither did his mother. As they reached the motorway, the first spots of rain began to fall, bringing the summer to an end.

*Truth or Dare* is a work of fiction. Any resemblance that characters may have to real people, either dead or living, is purely coincidental.

In the 1950s not much was known about autistic spectrum disorders, and treatment was uncertain. Fortunately, this is no longer the case. I would like to thank Andrew Nye, Fleur Birks and Martine Ives for their very helpful comments on the manuscript of *Truth or Dare*, and for sharing with me their insights into Aspergers Syndrome.

Celia Rees
July 1999

Celia Rees
# The Bailey Game

Every school has places that you can find if you want to, if you don't want people to see you, if you need somewhere private. That had been important in the Bailey Game – privacy and being secret.

The Bailey Game was vicious, it wrecked people's lives. But two years ago, it was all anyone in Alex's class thought or talked about. Until one terrifying day in early spring. What happened then should have been enough to stop anyone wanting to play the Game again – ever.

Now a new girl, Lauren Price, has arrived at the school. She is new, she is different, and she comes from somewhere else. That is enough. The Bailey Game is about to start.

Alex finds she has some tough choices to make in a world where being on the outside can be dangerous . . .

'This is a very exciting and disturbing tale which will hold the reader's interest right to the end. I highly recommend The Bailey Game.'
Michele Elliott, KIDSCAPE